# MORE MOUNTAIN MAN TRAIL BUILDERS

---

## MOUNTAIN MEN WHO BUILD

### BITTERROOT RIDGE TRAIL BUILDERS
### BOOK 2

## PEYTON LAWSON

Edited by Veronica Jauregui

Cover by Peyton Lawson

BEACHES AND TRAILS
PUBLISHING

# CONTENTS

# CARVED BY THE
# MOUNTAIN MAN

# 1

## FLOWERS AND FIREWOOD

**HALLIE**

The truck lurched to a stop outside the cabin, and I cursed as apple cider sloshed over the edge of the cup. The delivery order said to drop the mums at the house with the red mailbox—easy enough to find in a town this small. What it didn't mention was that the house came with a half-naked lumberjack fantasy chopping wood in the front yard.

I sat there like an idiot, gripping the steering wheel as my brain short-circuited.

He was huge. Broad shoulders that flexed with every swing of the axe, dark hair curled with sweat, and forearms that looked like they could split more than just firewood. The flannel shirt he'd discarded hung from a nearby fence post, leaving him in just worn jeans that sat low on his hips.

*Get it together, Hallie.* I was here to deliver flowers, not drool over the local wildlife.

I grabbed the arrangement of burnt orange mums from the

passenger seat and climbed out. My boots crunched on the gravel drive, but he didn't look up. The axe came down with a sharp crack that made me jump.

"Excuse me?" I called out, trying to sound professional instead of flustered. "Delivery for Walker Boone?"

The axe paused mid-swing. He straightened slowly, turning to face me, and I nearly dropped the flowers.

Christ. Up close, he was even more devastating. Dark eyes that looked right through me, a jaw shadowed with scruff, and a mouth that was currently pressed into a hard line. The kind of mouth that probably said dirty things when it wasn't scowling.

"You're late," he said, his voice gravelly and low.

I blinked. "I'm... what?"

"Festival started an hour ago. These were supposed to be there already."

Heat crawled up my neck. "I'm sorry, I had trouble finding—"

"Just leave them on the porch."

He turned back to the woodpile like I'd been dismissed. Like I was nothing more than an inconvenience.

*Rude much?*

I bit back the smart comment, trying to escape, and marched toward the porch. The mums were beautiful—carefully arranged with trailing ivy and miniature pumpkins that I'd spent twenty minutes perfecting this morning. They deserved better than to be dumped on some grump's doorstep.

I bent to set them down and knocked over the damn cider cup I'd somehow carried with me. Sticky liquid splashed across the wooden boards and my jeans.

"Shit!" The word slipped out before I could stop it.

Behind me, the chopping stopped again.

I crouched down, trying to clean up the mess with the napkins from my pocket, but it was useless. My hands were shaking—from embarrassment or something else entirely—and I was making it worse.

"Here."

A shadow fell over me. I looked up to find him standing there with a towel, still shirtless, still scowling, but holding it out like a peace offering.

Our fingers brushed when I took it, and electricity shot straight up my arm. His hands were calloused, warm, and bigger than they had any right to be. The kind of hands that could pin a woman down or work her apart with equal skill.

*Stop.*

"Thanks," I managed, not meeting his eyes.

I mopped up the cider as quickly as possible, hyperaware of him standing there. He smelled like wood shavings and sweat and something indefinably male that made my mouth go dry.

"The mums are nice," he said, quieter this time.

I glanced up in surprise. "Thanks. I grow them myself."

Something shifted in his expression, but before I could figure out what, he stepped back.

"I should get going," I babbled, standing too fast. "Festival to get to and all that."

He nodded once, already turning away.

I practically ran to my truck, tossing the towel in the back and climbing behind the wheel with shaking hands. In the rearview mirror, I watched him pick up the axe again, muscles bunching as he swung it down.

*Walker Boone.*

The name suited him—solid, uncompromising, a little bit dangerous. I tried to ignore the way it made my stomach flutter as I pulled out of the driveway.

Some men were meant to be looked at from a distance. Walker Boone was definitely one of them.

**WALKER**

I watched her truck disappear down the road and immediately wanted to punch myself in the face.

*Smooth, Walker. Real fucking smooth.*

She'd been nervous, flustered, and cute as hell trying to clean up that mess. And what had I done? Stood there like a caveman, grunting out one-word responses and scaring her off.

The flower girl. Hallie, according to the order form Avery had shown me last week. She was new in town—had opened the little flower shop next to Patterson's general store about a month ago. I'd been careful to avoid walking past it, because I'd seen her through the window once and known immediately that she was trouble.

The kind of trouble that made a man forget why he'd sworn off complications.

She was all soft curves and sunshine smiles, with honey-colored hair that looked like it would feel like silk between my fingers. Today, she'd been wearing jeans that hugged her hips and a sweater that did nothing to hide the fact that she was built like every fantasy I'd ever had.

And I'd been a complete ass to her.

I split another log with more force than necessary, trying to work off the frustration crawling under my skin. This was exactly why I avoided people. Especially women. Especially women who looked at me like they were seeing something worth looking at.

I'd learned that lesson the hard way.

The sound of gravel crunching made me look up, expecting to see her truck returning. Instead, my seven-year-old daughter came tearing around the side of the house like her hair was on fire.

"Daddy!" Avery skidded to a stop, grinning up at me with gap-toothed enthusiasm. "Did you meet the flower lady? Was she pretty? Did you ask her to the festival?"

I set down the axe and reached for my shirt. "Slow down, pumpkin. And why aren't you at Jenny's house?"

"Mrs. Morrison had to run errands, so she dropped me off early." Avery bounced on her toes, clearly bursting with energy. "So? Did you meet her?"

"I met her." I pulled the flannel over my head, noting the way Avery's eyes lit up. "She delivered the flowers. That's it."

"But did you *talk* to her? Like, really talk?"

"Avery—"

"Because I saw her at the store yesterday and she smells like vanilla and she has the prettiest laugh and Mrs. Patterson says she's single and—"

"That's enough." I used my dad voice, the one that usually got her attention. "What have I told you about matchmaking?"

Her face fell. "That you don't need a girlfriend because you have me."

"That's right." I knelt down to her level, softening my tone. "You're all I need, kiddo. We're good, just the two of us."

She nodded, but I could see the wheels still turning behind those brown eyes. Avery had her mother's stubborn streak and my protective instincts. It was a dangerous combination.

"Come on," I said, standing and ruffling her hair. "Let's get you some lunch before the festival."

We headed toward the house, but I caught her glancing back toward the road where Hallie's truck had disappeared.

Yeah. My daughter was definitely planning something.

And I had a sinking feeling that the pretty flower girl was about to become a much bigger problem than I'd bargained for.

## 2

---

# BONFIRES AND BULLSHIT

**HALLIE**

The Bitterroot Ridge Fall Festival looked like every small-town Pinterest board come to life. Hay bales stacked like makeshift seating, string lights draped between maple trees, and the smell of cinnamon donuts thick enough to make me dizzy. I'd been here two hours, manning my booth and watching families laugh over pumpkin picking, and I was finally starting to relax.

Until I saw him.

Walker stood behind the wood carving demonstration table, looking like he'd rather be anywhere else on earth. His jaw was locked tight, his shoulders rigid, and he was gripping a carving knife like it had personally offended him.

"More volunteers!" chirped Sally Patterson, the festival coordinator, appearing at my elbow with the enthusiasm of a caffeinated cheerleader. "Perfect timing, Hallie. We're short-handed at the carving booth."

My stomach dropped. "Oh, I don't really—"

"Nonsense! You have wonderful hands. I can always tell." She was already steering me toward the booth before I could protest. "Walker, meet your new partner. Hallie, Walker. You two will demonstrate basic carving techniques for the families."

Walker's eyes met mine across the table, and something hot and dangerous flickered there before his expression went carefully blank.

"Mrs. Patterson, I work better alone," he said, his voice low and controlled.

"Ridiculous. Teamwork makes the dream work!" Sally clapped her hands together like that settled everything. "I'll leave you two to get acquainted."

She bustled off, leaving me standing there like an idiot while Walker stared at me with all the warmth of a glacier.

"Look," I started, "if you don't want help, I can just—"

"You know how to carve?" His question cut through my rambling.

"Some. My dad taught me when I was little." I reached for one of the practice blocks, running my fingers over the smooth basswood. "Nothing fancy, but I can manage basic techniques."

He handed me a knife without a word, and our fingers brushed again. The same electric shock from this morning, but stronger now. More deliberate.

I tried to focus on the wood, but I could feel him watching as I made the first careful cuts. His presence was overwhelming—all heat and pine scent and controlled power that made my hands shake slightly.

"Your grip's wrong."

Before I could react, he was behind me, his chest brushing my back as he reached around to adjust my hold on the knife. His hands covered mine, calloused fingers guiding my movements, and I forgot how to breathe.

"Like this," he murmured, his voice rough and close to my ear. "Firm but flexible. Let the blade do the work."

The double meaning hit me like a slap, and heat flooded my cheeks. I turned my head slightly and found his face inches from mine, his dark eyes fixed on my mouth.

"Better?" I whispered.

His jaw tightened. "Much."

A family approached the booth, breaking the spell, and Walker stepped back so quickly that I almost stumbled. But for the next hour, we worked side by side, demonstrating cuts and helping kids carve simple pumpkins. Every accidental brush of our hands felt intentional. Every shared look lasted a beat too long.

"You're good at this," I said during a brief lull, watching him patiently guide a ten-year-old through shaping an owl's beak.

"Practice," he said simply.

"How long have you been carving?"

"Since I was younger than him." He nodded toward the boy. "My dad taught me."

There was something in his tone that made me want to ask more, but before I could, a woman with perfectly styled blonde hair and a practiced smile appeared at our table. She was maybe mid-thirties, with the kind of polished look that screamed city money and weekend trips to small towns.

"Well, hello there," she said, her gaze fixed entirely on Walker while completely ignoring me. "I don't suppose you give private lessons?"

I felt my back teeth clench.

Walker's expression didn't change, but I caught the way his

shoulders tensed. "I work through the community center. They have a schedule online."

"Oh, I'm sure we could work out something more... personal." She leaned across the table, giving him an excellent view down her low-cut sweater. "I'm very interested in learning about your... techniques."

The way she said it made my skin crawl. This wasn't about wood carving.

"He's busy," I said before I could stop myself.

Blonde hair turned to me with raised eyebrows, like she was just noticing I existed. "I'm sorry, and you are?"

"His partner," I said sweetly, then realized how that sounded. "For the booth. We're working together."

Her smile turned razor-sharp. "How nice. Well, when you're done playing teacher, I'll be around the festival. You seem like a man who knows how to handle his tools."

She sauntered away with an exaggerated sway of her hips, and I stared at the wood block in my hands, mortified by my own reaction.

"You didn't need to do that," Walker said quietly.

"I know. I just... she was being pushy."

"She was." He was looking at me with an expression I couldn't read. "But you handled it."

A group of teenagers approached before I could respond, and we fell back into the rhythm of teaching and demonstrating. But the tension between us had shifted, becoming something sharper and more charged.

As the sun started to set and families began packing up, I found myself reluctant to leave. Working beside Walker felt natural, despite the electric current that seemed to run between us whenever we got too close.

"Thank you," he said as we started cleaning up the tools. "For earlier. And for helping today."

"It was fun. I'd forgotten how much I enjoyed carving."

He paused, a block of wood halfway to the storage box. "You could come by the workshop sometime. If you wanted to practice."

My heart stuttered. "Your workshop?"

"Behind my cabin. I have better tools there."

I opened my mouth to say yes, then caught myself. This was dangerous territory. Walker Boone was the kind of man who could wreck a woman's carefully rebuilt life without even trying.

"I should probably—"

"Think about it," he said, his voice lower now, rougher. "But just so we're clear, Hallie—if you come, it won't be just about carvings."

The words hit me like a physical touch, sending heat spiraling through my body. I stared at him, lips parted, completely undone by the promise in his voice.

He packed up the last of the tools and walked away, leaving me standing there with my pulse racing and my carefully maintained walls crumbling around my feet.

*Shit.*


## WALKER

I made it exactly three steps before I wanted to turn around and take back every fucking word I'd just said.

*If you come, it won't be just about carvings.*

Christ. I might as well have carved "I want to fuck you" into the demonstration table. Real subtle, Walker.

But watching her all afternoon—the way she bit her lower lip when she concentrated, the soft sound she made when she cut herself and automatically reached for me to look at it, the fire in her eyes when she faced down that pushy blonde—had worn my control down to nothing.

And when that woman showed up, all predatory smiles and obvious intent, I wanted to grab Hallie and make it crystal clear who I was actually thinking about these days.

Which was insane. I didn't think about women. Hadn't since my marriage imploded and I'd learned that trusting someone with your heart was the fastest way to get it shattered. I had Avery to think about, a business to run, and a life that worked exactly the way it was. Simple. Controlled. Safe.

But Hallie...

Hallie had defended me without being asked. She'd called herself my partner with such fierce protectiveness that something primitive and possessive had roared to life in my chest.

And now I'd gone and opened my big mouth, making promises I had no business making to a woman who was clearly running from something herself. I'd seen the shadows in her eyes when she thought no one was looking, the way she flinched slightly when people got too loud or moved too fast.

She was broken in some way, just like me. Which should have been enough reason to stay the hell away.

Instead, it made me want to find whoever had hurt her and carve them into pieces.

"Daddy!"

Avery came barreling toward me through the crowd, her face sticky with caramel apple and her eyes bright with excitement.

"Did you see? Did you see Mrs. Patterson put you and the flower lady together?" She bounced on her toes, practically vibrating with glee. "I told her you needed a partner!"

I stopped walking. "You what?"

"I told her you were lonely and the flower lady was nice and maybe you could be friends!" She grabbed my hand, tugging me toward the parking area. "Was I right? Are you friends now?"

*Lonely.* My seven-year-old daughter thought I was lonely.

Hell, she wasn't wrong.

"Avery, what have I told you about—"

"I know, I know. No matchmaking. But I wasn't matchmaking! I was just... suggesting."

I opened my mouth to lecture her about the difference, then caught sight of Hallie walking to her truck. She moved with quick, nervous energy, like she was trying to escape something. Her hair had come loose from its ponytail during the afternoon, falling in soft waves around her shoulders, and even from this distance, I could see the flush on her cheeks.

She looked thoroughly rattled.

Good. At least I wasn't the only one.

"She's really pretty, isn't she?" Avery said, following my gaze. "And she smells like vanilla."

"How do you know what she smells like?"

"I went to her flower shop yesterday after school. Mrs. Morrison took me while she was getting her hair done." Avery grinned up at me. "She let me help arrange some roses. And she has a cat! A big orange one named Pumpkin."

Of course she did. The woman was basically sunshine and kittens wrapped up in curves that made my mouth water.

"Can we invite her for dinner?" Avery asked. "I could make my famous spaghetti."

"Your famous spaghetti comes from a box."

"It's still famous! Please, Daddy? She seemed sad. I think she needs friends."

I looked at my daughter—all gap-toothed hope and innocent scheming—and felt my resolve cracking. She was right about one thing. Hallie had seemed sad. Lonely. And despite every instinct screaming at me to keep my distance, I wanted to know why.

"We'll see," I said, which was parent-speak for 'absolutely not, but I don't want to crush your dreams right now.'

Avery beamed like I'd promised her a pony.

As we walked to the truck, I caught one last glimpse of Hallie climbing into her beat-up Honda. She sat there for a moment, hands gripping the steering wheel, and even from here I could see the way her shoulders rose and fell with deep breaths.

She was thinking about what I'd said. About coming to the workshop.

About what would happen if she did.

The smart thing would be to hope she stayed away. The safe thing would be to forget the way she'd felt in my arms, all soft warmth and nervous energy.

But as I watched her drive away, I found myself hoping she was braver than I was.

Because despite every wall I'd built, every lesson I'd learned, I wanted her to come.

I wanted her to take the risk, I was too much of a coward to take myself.

# 3

## ONLY ONE BED

HALLIE

At three in the morning, the pipe burst with a noise like a mini explosion. I jolted awake to the crash of water hitting my bedroom floor, followed by the sick realization that everything I owned was about to be soaked. My landlord's ancient plumbing had finally given up, and judging by the steady stream pouring through my ceiling, it wasn't going to be a quick fix.

By dawn, I was standing in my flooded apartment wearing yesterday's clothes and trying not to cry. The water had destroyed my bed, my dresser, and most of my winter clothes. Everything smelled like mildew and broken dreams.

"Oh, honey, no." Mrs. Patterson appeared in my doorway like a flannel-clad fairy godmother, taking in the damage with horrified eyes. "You can't stay here."

"It's fine," I lied, wrapping my arms around myself. "I'll figure something out."

"Nonsense. You're coming home with me until—"

"Hallie!"

We both turned to find Avery Boone racing up the stairs, her backpack bouncing and her face bright with excitement. Behind her, moving much more slowly, was Walker.

My heart did something complicated at the sight of him. He was wearing work clothes—faded jeans and a flannel that stretched across his broad chest—and his dark hair was still messy from sleep. He looked rumpled and warm and exactly like the kind of trouble I'd spent all night trying not to think about.

"What happened?" he asked, taking in my soaked apartment with a frown.

"Pipe burst," Mrs. Patterson explained. "Poor thing's lost everything."

"Not everything," I protested weakly. "Just... most things."

Avery pushed past us into the apartment, her eyes wide as she took in the destruction. "Wow. It's like a swimming pool in here."

"Avery, get back," Walker said sharply. "The ceiling could come down."

He was right. The water damage was worse than I'd initially thought, and the ancient building groaned ominously with every gust of wind.

"You can stay with us!" Avery announced, spinning around to face me with the kind of enthusiasm only seven-year-olds could muster. "We have a guest room!"

My eyes flew to Walker, who looked like he'd been punched in the gut.

"That's very sweet, sweetheart, but I'm sure your dad—"

"It's not a problem," Walker said quietly, his voice carefully controlled. "The guest room is... available."

Mrs. Patterson beamed. "Perfect! Crisis solved."

I wanted to argue, to insist I could handle this myself, but the truth was I couldn't. My savings account was laughable, and the only hotel within fifty miles was booked solid with leaf-peepers. I was well and truly stuck.

"Just for a night or two," I said quickly. "Until I can figure out something else."

Walker nodded once, but I caught the way his jaw tightened. He wasn't happy about this arrangement either.

Which made two of us.

An hour later, I was standing in Walker's cabin with a garbage bag full of salvaged clothes and the sinking realization that I'd made a terrible mistake. The cabin was smaller than I'd expected —cozy in a way that meant there was nowhere to hide. The living room flowed into the kitchen, which opened onto a loft where I could see Avery's bedroom. Everything was wood and stone and masculine comfort.

"Guest room's this way," Walker said, leading me down a short hallway.

He opened a door, and I bit back a laugh. The "guest room" was barely bigger than a closet, with a twin bed shoved against one wall and boxes stacked everywhere else.

"I know it's not much," he said, running a hand through his hair. "I don't really have guests."

"It's perfect," I lied, because what else could I say?

But as the day wore on, perfect became complicated. Walker's cabin was his sanctuary, and my presence clearly threw off his carefully controlled routine. He kept finding excuses to stay outside—chopping wood, fixing something on the porch, anything to avoid being in the same room as me.

I tried to make myself invisible, curling up on the couch with a book while Avery chattered about school, pumpkins and whether I liked hot chocolate with marshmallows or whipped cream. But every time Walker came inside, the air seemed to thicken with tension.

By evening, I was ready to sleep in my car.

"I should probably find somewhere else to stay," I said as we finished dinner. "I don't want to impose."

"You're not imposing," Avery said quickly. "Right, Daddy?"

Walker's dark eyes met mine across the table. "Right."

But his voice was tight, and I could see the muscle jumping in his jaw. He wanted me gone as much as I wanted to leave.

Later, after Avery had been tucked into bed and Walker had disappeared into his workshop, I tried to settle into the tiny guest room. The twin bed was comfortable enough, but the walls were thin, and I could hear every sound Walker made moving around the cabin.

The creak of floorboards. The soft thud of the refrigerator door. The low rumble of his voice as he talked to someone on the phone about a job.

It was intimate in a way that made my skin feel too tight.

I was finally starting to drift off when I heard his bedroom door open. Footsteps in the hallway. A pause outside my door that lasted long enough to make my breath catch.

Then silence.

I lay there in the dark, hyperaware of him just a few feet away, separated by nothing but drywall and good intentions. The memory of his hands on mine at the festival replayed in my mind, along with the rough promise in his voice.

*If you come, it won't be just about carvings.*

I was here now. In his space, in his life, in dangerous proximity to everything I'd sworn I wouldn't want.

And God help me, I was starting to think the carving was the least of my problems.

## WALKER

She was a mere three feet away from me, and it was killing me.

I lay in my bed, staring at the ceiling and trying not to think about the fact that Hallie Blake was sleeping in my house. In my space. Close enough that I could hear the soft sounds she made as she shifted in the too-small bed.

This was a mistake. A huge, catastrophic mistake that I'd agreed to because my daughter had looked at me with those big brown eyes, and I'd been too much of a coward to disappoint her.

Or maybe I'd agreed because some twisted part of me wanted Hallie here. Wanted to know what it felt like to have her warm presence filling the cold corners of my life.

Either way, I was fucked.

I'd spent the day hyper-aware of her every movement. The way she curled up on my couch like she belonged there. The soft laugh she gave Avery when my daughter told her ridiculous jokes. The careful way she moved through my kitchen, like she was trying not to disturb anything.

She was trying to be invisible, and it was driving me insane.

A soft thud from the guest room made me freeze. Then another. The unmistakable sound of someone moving around restlessly.

She couldn't sleep either.

I should stay in bed. Should ignore whatever was happening three feet away and mind my own damn business. But before I could talk myself out of it, I was getting up and padding quietly to my door.

I stood there like a creep, listening to the sounds of her tossing and turning. The bed was too small for her—I'd known that when I offered the room, but it was all I had. She had to be uncomfortable as hell.

*Just check on her. Make sure she's okay.*

I cracked the door open and immediately regretted it. The hallway was dark, but I could see the guest room door was ajar, and through the gap, I caught a glimpse of long, bare legs tangled in sheets.

She was wearing something short. Something that had ridden up as she moved, exposing the curve of her thigh and making my mouth go dry.

*Move away. Go back to bed. Don't be a fucking pervert.*

But I couldn't seem to make my feet work. I stood there frozen, watching her shift restlessly, and every protective instinct I had roared to life. She was uncomfortable. Probably cold. Definitely not getting any sleep in that ridiculous excuse for a bed.

Before I could think it through, I was knocking softly on her door.

"Hallie? You okay?"

The movement stopped. Then her voice, soft and slightly breathless: "I'm fine. Sorry if I woke you."

"You didn't." I pushed the door open a little wider. "Can't sleep?"

She sat up, pulling the sheet around herself, and even in the dim light, I could see the flush on her cheeks. Her hair was messed up from tossing and turning, and she looked rumpled and vulnerable and so fucking beautiful it hurt.

"The bed's a little small," she admitted.

I leaned against the doorframe, trying to look casual instead of like a man on the edge of doing something stupid. "My bed's bigger."

The words hung in the air between us, loaded with implications neither of us was ready to face.

"Walker..." she started, but I could hear the uncertainty in her voice. The want.

"I'm not suggesting anything," I said quickly, which was a lie. I was suggesting everything. "Just that you might actually get some sleep."

She bit her lower lip, considering, and I had to grip the door-frame to keep from crossing the room and kissing her senseless.

"It would just be sleeping," she said finally.

"Just sleeping," I agreed, even though we both knew it was bullshit.

Five minutes later, she was standing next to my king-size bed wearing an oversized t-shirt that hit her mid-thigh and looking like every fantasy I'd ever had. The shirt was thin enough that I could see the outline of her breasts, the hint of her nipples beneath the soft cotton.

I was going to die. Actually die.

"Which side do you prefer?" she asked, her voice carefully neutral.

"Doesn't matter." I pulled back the covers, trying to act like this was normal. Like I regularly shared my bed with gorgeous women who smelled like vanilla and made me want to forget every hard lesson I'd learned about trust.

She climbed in carefully, staying as far to her side as possible. I did the same, but the bed that had felt huge when I slept alone suddenly seemed tiny with both of us in it.

"Thank you," she whispered into the darkness. "For letting me stay. For everything."

"It's nothing."

"It's not nothing to me."

The sincerity in her voice did something dangerous to my chest. I turned toward her without thinking, and found her facing me in the dim light filtering through the curtains. Her eyes were wide and uncertain, her lips slightly parted.

The space between us felt electric. Charged with possibility and want and all the reasons we should keep our distance.

"Hallie," I said, her name coming out rougher than I intended.

"Yeah?"

"You should get some sleep."

She nodded, but neither of us moved. Neither of us looked away.

"Walker?"

"Yeah?"

"What made you so careful about letting people in?"

The question hit me like cold water. I rolled onto my back, staring at the ceiling, and felt all the walls I'd carefully built slam back into place.

"People leave," I said simply. "Rebecca, my ex-wife, decided that small-town life wasn't enough. That Avery and I weren't enough."

"I'm sorry."

"Don't be. It taught me what I needed to know."

"Did it?"

I turned to look at her again, and the compassion in her eyes nearly undid me. "Yeah. It did."

"Is that why you don't take chances on people?"

The question was quiet, careful, but it hit right at the heart of everything I was trying not to feel.

"Among other reasons."

"What are the other reasons?"

*Because women like you deserve better than broken men like me. Because I don't know how to be what anyone needs. Because the last time I let someone in, they took everything and left me bleeding.*

"Go to sleep, Hallie."

She was quiet for so long I thought she'd given up. Then: "For what it's worth, I think she's an idiot."

The words hit me square in the chest, and I had to close my eyes against the sudden, fierce want that crashed through me. Not just physical want, though there was plenty of that. But something deeper. More dangerous.

The want to believe her. To trust her. To let her close enough to find out if she meant it.

I lay there listening to her breathing even out as she finally fell asleep, and knew I was in serious trouble. Because despite every wall I'd built, every lesson I'd learned, Hallie Blake was already closer than anyone had been in years.

And the terrifying thing was, I didn't want her to move away.

# 4

## ROUGH EDGES

**HALLIE**

I woke up warm.

Not just comfortable warm, but surrounded-by-a-furnace warm. It took my sleep-addled brain a moment to realize that the furnace was Walker, and that sometime during the night, we'd migrated toward each other like magnets.

His arm was draped over my waist, heavy and possessive. My back was pressed against his chest, and I could feel every breath he took, every beat of his heart. His hand had somehow found its way under my t-shirt, his palm flat against my stomach, and the skin-to-skin contact was making me dizzy.

This was supposed to be just sleeping.

I should move. Should carefully extract myself before he woke up, and we had to pretend this hadn't happened. But his body was solid and warm behind me, and for the first time in months, I felt completely safe.

So I stayed still and let myself have this. Just for a moment.

His breathing changed, becoming less deep, less even. He was waking up. I felt the exact moment he realized how we were positioned, because his entire body went rigid.

But he didn't move away.

His thumb brushed across my skin, just once, and I bit back a gasp. The touch was light, almost accidental, but it sent electricity shooting through my entire nervous system.

"Hallie," he said, his voice rough with sleep and something darker.

"Yeah?"

"I should move."

"You should."

But neither of us moved. His hand stayed splayed across my stomach, and I stayed pressed against him, both of us breathing carefully in the gray morning light.

"This is a bad idea," he said.

"Terrible idea," I agreed.

His lips brushed the back of my neck, so softly I might have imagined it. "Really fucking bad."

I turned in his arms before I could think better of it, and suddenly we were face to face, his dark eyes fixed on mine with an intensity that made my breath catch. His hair was messed up from sleep, and there was stubble shadowing his jaw. He looked rumpled and dangerous and like every mistake I wanted to make.

"Walker," I whispered.

His gaze dropped to my mouth, and I saw him swallow hard. "I should get up. Make coffee. Check on Avery."

"You should."

But instead of moving away, his hand came up to trace the line of my jaw. His thumb brushed across my lower lip, and I couldn't stop the soft sound that escaped me.

"Fuck," he breathed, and leaned closer.

A door slammed somewhere in the house, followed by Avery's voice calling out, "Daddy! I'm hungry!"

We sprang apart like we'd been electrocuted. Walker was out of bed and pulling on a shirt before I could even sit up, his movements sharp and controlled.

"I'll get breakfast started," he said without looking at me. "Take your time."

He left the room like it was on fire, and I flopped back against the pillows, my heart racing and my skin still tingling from his touch.

*Get it together, Hallie. This is exactly what you came here to avoid.*

But as I lay there listening to the sounds of Walker making breakfast and Avery chattering about her plans for the day, I couldn't shake the feeling that I was already in way too deep.

Twenty minutes later, I finally made it to the kitchen, where Walker was standing at the stove with Avery bouncing beside him.

"Can you make them into shapes?" Avery was asking hopefully.

"I don't think so kid. I just know how to make the round ones." Walker looked up when I entered, his dark eyes still heated from this morning.

"Morning. Avery wants shaped pancakes."

"What kind of shapes?" I asked, grateful for the distraction from the tension crackling between us. "Pumpkins!" Avery grinned.

"Like the decorations we saw yesterday!" I moved to the counter, careful not to brush against Walker as I reached for the spatula.

"I think I can manage that."

"You know how to make shaped pancakes?" Walker asked, something soft in his voice.

"My dad taught me when I was little. Used to make them for

special occasions." I poured batter into the pan, guiding it into a rough pumpkin shape.

"Nothing fancy, but..."

"It's perfect," he said quietly, and when I looked up, he wasn't looking at the pancake. He was looking at me. Avery clapped as the first pumpkin pancake came off the griddle.

"It really looks like a pumpkin! Can you make one for Daddy too?"

"Sure, kiddo." I poured another, hyperaware of Walker watching my hands as I worked.

"Everyone deserves a special pancake."

THE POWER WENT OUT JUST as the first snow started to fall.

I was in the living room, trying to read a book and absolutely not thinking about this morning, when the lights flickered and died. Outside, the wind had picked up, and fat snowflakes were swirling past the windows with increasing intensity.

"Well, shit," Walker said from the kitchen.

"Daddy said a bad word!" Avery announced gleefully from her spot on the floor, where she'd been coloring.

"Sorry, pumpkin." Walker appeared in the doorway, running a hand through his hair. "Looks like we're going to lose power for a while. The storm came in faster than they predicted."

As if to emphasize his point, the wind howled around the cabin, rattling the windows. The temperature had already started to drop, and without the electric heat, it was only going to get colder.

"Do you have a generator?" I asked.

"It's in the shop. Broke down last week." Walker moved to the fireplace, kneeling down to start building a fire. "We'll be fine. This cabin's well-insulated, and the fireplace puts out good heat."

I watched him work, mesmerized by the efficient way he arranged the kindling and logs. His hands were steady and sure, and within minutes, flames were crackling in the hearth.

"There," he said, sitting back on his heels. "That should help."

But as the evening wore on, it became clear that the fireplace alone wasn't going to be enough. The storm had turned into a full-blown blizzard, and the temperature inside the cabin continued to drop despite the fire.

Avery had crawled under a pile of blankets on the couch, but I could see her shivering. Walker kept feeding the fire, but his jaw was tight with worry.

"Maybe we should all sleep in the living room tonight," I suggested. "Close to the fire."

Walker nodded. "Good idea. I'll get the mattresses."

We set up a makeshift campsite in front of the fireplace, dragging down pillows and every blanket in the house. Avery thought it was a grand adventure, chattering excitedly as we arranged our sleeping area.

But as the night deepened and the fire burned lower, the cold became impossible to ignore.

"I can't feel my toes," Avery whispered from her nest of blankets.

Walker was beside her in an instant, pulling her against his side and wrapping them both in his sleeping bag. "Better?"

She nodded, but I could see she was still shivering. I was too, despite the layers I'd piled on.

"Come here," Walker said quietly, meeting my eyes across the small space.

I hesitated. We'd barely managed to keep our hands off each

other this morning when we were warm and comfortable. Being pressed together for body heat was asking for trouble.

But Avery was cold, and I was cold, and Walker was looking at me with an expression that said he was thinking about practical survival, not whatever had almost happened between us earlier.

I crawled over to them, and Walker lifted his arm to include me in their makeshift shelter. Suddenly, I was pressed against his side, with Avery between us, all of us sharing warmth and breath and the intimate space created by the sleeping bag.

"Better?" Walker asked, his voice low and rough.

I nodded, not trusting myself to speak. Being this close to him was torture. I could smell his skin, feel the steady rise and fall of his chest, and sense the controlled tension in his body.

"Tell us a story, Daddy," Avery mumbled sleepily.

"What kind of story?"

"A princess story. But with woodcarving."

Walker chuckled, the sound vibrating through his chest. "Once upon a time, there was a princess who could carve magic into wood..."

His voice was soft and hypnotic as he spun a tale about a princess who carved doorways to other worlds and a grumpy woodsman who tried to stop her. I found myself relaxing against his warmth, lulled by the rumble of his voice and the crackling of the fire.

Avery fell asleep first, her small body going limp between us. But I stayed awake, hyperaware of every place my body touched Walker's. His hand had somehow found its way to my hair, his fingers threading through the strands in a gesture that felt unconscious but intimate.

"You're good at that," I whispered. "The storytelling."

"Lots of practice. Avery's been demanding bedtime stories since she could talk."

"She's lucky to have you."

His hand stilled in my hair. "Sometimes I wonder if she'd be better off with someone who knew what the hell they were doing."

"You're kidding, right?" I turned to look at him, careful not to wake Avery. "Walker, you're an amazing father. She adores you."

"She deserves better than a dad who can barely handle having a conversation with another adult."

The pain in his voice made my chest ache. "Is that what you think? That you're not enough?"

"I know I'm not enough. Rebecca made that pretty clear."

I wanted to argue, to tell him his ex-wife was an idiot who didn't deserve either of them. But something in his expression stopped me. This wasn't about Rebecca. This was about something deeper, some fundamental belief he had about himself.

"You're wrong," I said simply.

He looked at me for a long moment, his dark eyes unreadable in the firelight. Then, slowly, his hand cupped my cheek.

"Hallie," he said, my name rough and desperate on his lips.

I knew he was going to kiss me. Could see the intention in his eyes, the way his gaze dropped to my mouth. Every rational part of my brain screamed at me to pull away, to remember all the reasons this was a bad idea.

Instead, I leaned closer.

His lips were soft and warm and tasted like everything I'd been trying not to want. The kiss was gentle at first, almost hesitant, like he was giving me a chance to change my mind.

I didn't want to change my mind. I wanted to sink into this moment and forget about everything except the way he touched me like I was something precious.

But then Avery stirred between us, mumbling in her sleep, and reality crashed back in. We broke apart, breathing hard, and I saw my own confusion and want reflected in his eyes.

"We can't," he said quietly.

"I know."

But neither of us moved away. We lay there in the flickering firelight, too close and not close enough, until exhaustion finally pulled me under.

## WALKER

I didn't sleep.

I lay there holding Hallie and my daughter, listening to their breathing and trying not to think about how right this felt. How complete. Like something I'd been missing without knowing it had finally clicked into place.

Which was dangerous as hell.

I'd kissed her. Actually kissed her, with my seven-year-old daughter sleeping between us and a blizzard raging outside. I'd lost my mind completely.

But Christ, she'd tasted like everything I'd forgotten I wanted. Sweet and warm and completely willing. For a moment, the world had narrowed down to nothing but her soft mouth and the little sound she'd made when I'd deepened the kiss.

I was so fucked.

When morning finally came, gray and cold with snow still falling steadily outside, Hallie extracted herself carefully from our tangle of limbs. She didn't meet my eyes as she padded to the kitchen to start coffee on the gas stove.

Avery woke up chattering about the storm and how cool it was to camp inside, oblivious to the tension crackling between the adults. I was grateful for her chatter—it gave me something to focus on besides the way Hallie's hair looked sleep-mussed or the memory of how she'd felt in my arms.

"Power's still out," I said unnecessarily, checking my phone. "Probably be out most of the day."

"That's okay," Hallie said, still not looking at me. "I should probably check on my apartment anyway. See how bad the damage is."

She was running. I could see it in the careful way she moved, the distance she was maintaining. And I should let her run. It should make it easy for her to leave before this got any more complicated.

Instead, I found myself saying, "Roads are blocked. You're not going anywhere until the plows come through."

She finally looked at me then, and I saw a flash of something that might have been relief before she looked away again.

The day passed in careful avoidance. We played board games with Avery, read books, and made meals on the gas stove. But every accidental touch, every shared glance felt loaded with the memory of last night.

By evening, the power was back on and the roads were being cleared. Hallie could leave if she wanted to.

She didn't.

After Avery went to bed, I found myself in my workshop, hands busy with the piece of basswood I'd been carving. It was supposed to be a simple practice piece, but under my hands, it was becoming something else.

A flower. Delicate petals, careful detail work that required all my concentration. The kind of thing I'd never carved before, because I'd never had a reason to.

Now I did.

I worked until my hands cramped, until every petal was perfect, every line exactly where it should be. Then I set it carefully on my workbench and stared at it.

It was beautiful. And completely useless.

What the hell was I supposed to do with a carved flower? Give it to her like some lovesick teenager? Leave it on her pillow with a note?

The whole thing was ridiculous. I was a grown man, not some kid with a crush. I had responsibilities, a daughter to think about, a life that didn't have room for complications like feelings.

But as I turned off the workshop light and headed back to the house, the flower came with me.

I found Hallie in the kitchen, cleaning up the dinner dishes. She'd changed into another oversized t-shirt, and her hair was pulled back in a messy bun that made me want to tug it loose.

"You don't have to do that," I said.

"I want to help." She glanced at me, then away. "It's the least I can do."

"Hallie—"

"I know what you're going to say," she interrupted, turning to face me. "About last night. It was just the situation, right? The cold, the storm. It didn't mean anything."

She was giving me an out. A way to pretend the kiss hadn't happened, that the want I'd seen in her eyes was just my imagination.

I should take it. Should agree and let us both off the hook.

"Right," I said instead. "It didn't mean anything."

Something flickered across her face—disappointment? Hurt? —before she nodded. "Good. I'm glad we're on the same page."

But we weren't on the same page. We weren't even reading the same book.

Later, after she'd gone to bed, I stood outside her door holding the carved flower and feeling like an idiot. This was insane. I was acting like a man half my age, carving gifts for a woman who'd just made it clear she wasn't interested.

I should throw the damn thing away. Should go to bed and forget this whole thing ever happened.

Instead, I opened her door quietly and left the flower on her pillow.

She was asleep, curled on her side with one hand tucked under her cheek. In the dim light from the hallway, she looked young and vulnerable, and so beautiful it made my chest ache.

I stood there longer than I should have, memorizing the curve of her shoulder, the way her hair spilled across the pillow. Storing up the image for later, when she was gone and my bed felt too big again.

Then I closed the door and walked away, leaving behind the only honest thing I'd done all day.

# 5

## CARVED BY HIM

**HALLIE**

I found the flower when I woke up.

It sat on my pillow like a whispered secret, carved from pale wood with such delicate detail it looked almost real. Each petal was perfect, every curve exactly where it should be, and when I picked it up, it was warm from the morning light streaming through the window.

Walker had made this. Had spent hours carving something beautiful just for me, then left it like a ghost of everything he couldn't say.

My hands shook as I traced the smooth petals. This wasn't just wood. This was a confession. A promise. A question mark hanging in the air between us.

I should give it back. Should march into the kitchen where I could hear him making coffee and tell him this was too much, too fast, too everything.

Instead, I pressed it to my chest and closed my eyes, letting myself feel the weight of what he'd given me.

The kitchen was warm and bright when I finally emerged, dressed in jeans and a sweater that suddenly felt too conservative. Walker stood at the counter with his back to me, shoulders tense beneath his flannel shirt.

"Thank you," I said quietly.

He went still, coffee mug halfway to his lips. "For what?"

I held up the flower, and he turned slowly to face me. His dark eyes were guarded, but I could see the uncertainty there. The fear that I'd reject this small piece of his heart he'd offered.

"It's beautiful," I said.

"It's just a practice piece."

"No, it's not." I stepped closer, and his jaw tightened. "It's the most beautiful thing anyone's ever made for me."

Something raw and hungry flashed across his face before he looked away. "Hallie—"

"Where's Avery?"

"Sleepover at Jenny's house. Won't be back until tomorrow."

The words hung between us, loaded with possibility. We were alone. Completely, utterly alone for the first time since I'd arrived.

I set the flower carefully on the counter and moved closer. "Walker."

"This is a bad idea," he said, but his voice was rough, desperate.

"I know."

"You should stay away from me."

"I know that too."

I was close enough now to see the pulse jumping in his throat, to smell the scent of wood shavings and coffee that clung to his skin. His hands gripped the counter behind him like he was anchoring himself.

"I'm not good at this," he said. "At whatever this is."

"What do you think this is?"

His eyes met mine, dark and intense and full of everything he wasn't saying. "Dangerous."

I reached up and touched his face, feeling the scratch of stubble against my palm. "Maybe I like dangerous."

He caught my wrist, his grip gentle but firm. "You don't know what you're asking for."

"Then show me."

The words were barely out of my mouth before he moved. One moment I was standing in front of him, and the next I was pressed against the counter, his body caging me in, his mouth crashing down on mine.

This wasn't like the gentle kiss by the fire. This was desperation and want, and months of careful control finally snapping. His hands tangled in my hair, angling my head so he could deepen the kiss, and I melted against him.

He tasted like coffee and need and something darker that made me want to crawl inside him. When his teeth caught my lower lip, I gasped, and he swallowed the sound like he was starving for it.

"Hallie," he breathed against my mouth. "Christ, what are you doing to me?"

"Whatever you want," I whispered back, and felt him shudder.

His hands found the hem of my sweater, fingers skimming across my skin, and I arched into his touch. I'd forgotten what it felt like to want someone this much. To need their hands on you like you needed air.

"Please," I managed.

He pulled back just far enough to look at me, his eyes dark and wild. "You sure?"

"I've never been more sure of anything."

He lifted me onto the counter in one smooth motion, stepping between my legs and kissing me again. His hands roamed over my body with reverent urgency, like he was trying to memorize every curve.

"You're so fucking beautiful," he murmured against my throat. "Been thinking about this since the moment I saw you."

His confession sent heat spiraling through me. "Just thinking?"

"Dreaming. Obsessing." His mouth found the sensitive spot below my ear, and I gasped. "You have no idea what you do to me."

I could feel what I did to him pressed hard against my thigh, and it made me bold. My hands found the buttons of his shirt, working them open with shaking fingers.

"Hallie." My name was a warning and a prayer.

"I need to touch you," I said. "Please."

He helped me push the shirt off his shoulders, and I ran my hands over his chest, memorizing the feel of warm skin and hard muscle. He had scars—thin white lines across his ribs, a jagged mark on his shoulder—and I traced each one with gentle fingers.

"Beautiful," I whispered, and he made a sound low in his throat.

"Not beautiful. Broken."

I looked up at him, seeing the vulnerability in his eyes. "No. Strong. Survivor."

Something cracked in his expression, and then he was kissing me again, deeper this time, more desperate. His hands found the button of my jeans, and I lifted my hips to help him slide them down my legs.

"Bedroom," he said, but his voice was strained.

"Here," I said, pulling him closer. "I can't wait."

He groaned, his forehead dropping to rest against mine. "You're going to kill me."

"Good way to go?"

His laugh was rough and breathless. "The best."

He lifted me again, carrying me to his bedroom like I weighed nothing. The bed was unmade, sheets still tangled, and the sight of it made my pulse race.

He set me down gently beside the bed, his hands framing my face. "Last chance to change your mind."

"Stop giving me outs," I said, reaching for his belt. "I want this. I want you."

His control finally shattered. He kissed me hard and hungry while his hands made quick work of my remaining clothes. When I stood naked before him, he stepped back to look at me, his gaze so intense it felt like a physical touch.

"Perfect," he breathed. "You're perfect."

I should have felt self-conscious, standing there exposed while he was still half-dressed. Instead, I felt powerful. Beautiful. Wanted in a way I'd never experienced before.

"Your turn," I said, reaching for his jeans.

He helped me undress him, and when he stood naked before me, I couldn't help but stare. He was magnificent—all lean muscle and rough edges and controlled power. And he was hard for me, so hard it had to hurt.

"Come here," he said softly.

I moved into his arms, gasping at the feeling of skin against skin. He was warm and solid and everything I'd been craving without knowing it.

He laid me back on the bed with gentle hands, following me down to press kisses along my throat, my collarbone, the curve of my breast. Every touch was deliberate, worshipful, like he was trying to carve the memory into his skin.

"So soft," he murmured against my stomach. "So sweet."

His mouth moved lower, and I arched beneath him, lost in sensation. He knew exactly how to touch me, how to make me gasp and writhe and beg for more.

"Walker, please," I whispered.

"Please what?" His voice was rough with want.

"I need you. All of you."

He moved back up my body, settling between my thighs, and I could feel him there, hard and ready. But he didn't move, just looked down at me with something like wonder in his eyes.

"You sure?" he asked one more time.

"Yes," I breathed. "Please, yes."

He entered me slowly, carefully, giving me time to adjust. The stretch was perfect, overwhelming, and I wrapped my legs around his hips to pull him deeper.

"Fuck," he gasped. "Hallie, you feel..."

"Perfect," I finished for him. "You feel perfect."

He began to move then, slow and deep, and I lost myself in the rhythm. This wasn't just sex—it was something deeper, more primal. Like we were claiming each other, marking territory neither of us had known we wanted to defend.

"Look at me," he said when I closed my eyes. "I want to see you."

I opened my eyes and found him watching me intently, his face tight with concentration and something that looked almost like pain.

"So beautiful," he said, his thumb tracing my lower lip. "Especially when you're trying so hard not to come."

The words pushed me closer to the edge, and I could feel my climax building. He seemed to sense it too, because his movements became more urgent, more desperate.

"Come for me," he whispered. "Let me feel you."

I shattered around him with a cry that he swallowed with his mouth. The pleasure was overwhelming, perfect, and I clung to him as wave after wave crashed through me.

He followed me over a moment later, my name on his lips like a prayer, and collapsed against me with a shuddering breath.

We lay there afterward, tangled together in the afternoon light, and I traced patterns on his chest while he played with my hair.

I tilted my head to look at him. "Any regrets?"

His arms tightened around me. "Only that we waited so long."

## WALKER

She was going to destroy me.

I lay there holding her, feeling her soft breathing against my chest, and knew with absolute certainty that I was fucked. Not just physically, though that had been mind-blowing. But emotionally, completely, irrevocably fucked.

Because this wasn't just sex. This was Hallie curled against me like she belonged there, her hair spilling across my pillow, her body warm in my arms. This was everything I'd sworn I didn't want and exactly what I'd been missing without knowing it.

She'd been perfect. Responsive and eager and so goddamn beautiful it hurt to look at her. The way she'd touched me, like I was something precious instead of something broken. The sounds she'd made when I'd taken her apart with my hands and mouth.

I was already getting hard again just thinking about it.

"What are you thinking about?" she murmured against my chest.

"You," I said honestly. "How perfect you felt."

She lifted her head to look at me, her eyes still soft and dazed from sex. "Felt, "as in past tense?"

"Feel," I corrected, rolling her beneath me. "How perfect you feel."

I kissed her slowly this time, savoring the taste of her, the way she melted beneath me. She was already getting aroused again—I could feel it in the way her breathing changed, the way she arched into my touch.

"Again?" she whispered.

"Again," I confirmed, settling between her thighs. "I'm nowhere near done with you."

The second time was slower, deeper. I took my time exploring every inch of her body, learning what made her gasp and writhe and beg. She was vocal, unashamed in her pleasure, and every sound she made went straight to my cock.

When I finally entered her again, she was so wet and ready that I nearly lost control immediately. But I forced myself to go slow, to savor every moment of being inside her.

"You're mine," I said without thinking, the words ripped from somewhere deep in my chest.

Her eyes flew open, meeting mine with an intensity that stole my breath. "Yes," she whispered. "Yours."

The possessiveness that roared through me was primal, over-whelming. I'd never felt anything like it—this need to claim, to mark, to make sure everyone knew she belonged to me.

I fucked her harder, deeper, until she was crying out my name and clawing at my back. When she came, it was with an intensity that left her shaking, and I followed her over with a growl that came from my very soul.

Afterward, we lay tangled together as the afternoon light faded into evening. She traced the scars on my chest with gentle fingers, and I told her about each one. The knife cut from when I was learning to carve. The burn from helping fight a wildfire three summers ago. The jagged mark on my shoulder from a climbing accident when I was young and stupid.

"You've lived a lot of life," she said.

"Some of it good, some of it not so good."

"What about this?" She gestured between us. "Good or not so good?"

I caught her hand, bringing it to my lips to press a kiss to her palm. "The best."

She smiled, soft and real, and something settled in my chest. Something that felt dangerously like contentment.

"We should probably get up," she said eventually. "Avery will be home soon."

I groaned, burying my face in her neck. "Five more minutes."

"Five more minutes and we'll be naked when your seven-year-old walks through the door."

"Good point." But I didn't move. Couldn't make myself let go of this moment, this perfect bubble of peace we'd created.

"Walker?"

"Yeah?"

"Thank you. For the flower. For this. For making me feel..."

"What?"

"Wanted," she said quietly. "It's been a long time since I felt wanted."

The vulnerability in her voice made my chest ache. I pulled back to look at her, seeing the shadows that sometimes flickered in her eyes.

"You are wanted," I said fiercely. "So fucking wanted you have no idea."

She kissed me then, soft and sweet, and I poured everything I couldn't say into the kiss. All the words that were too big, too dangerous, too soon.

When we finally got up and dressed, I felt the loss of her skin against mine like a physical ache. But I watched her move around my bedroom, pulling on her clothes, and felt something I hadn't experienced in years.

Hope.

Maybe this could work. Maybe I could be what she needed, and she could be what I'd given up believing in.

Maybe this time, I wouldn't end up broken.

But as I watched her straighten the bed with careful hands, I caught her wince slightly as she moved. A reminder of what we'd done, of how thoroughly I'd claimed her.

And for the first time since she'd walked into my life, I let myself believe that maybe she'd claimed me right back.

# 6

## DON'T GET ATTACHED

HALLIE

I woke up alone in my small apartment above the flower shop.

The pipes had been fixed, the water damage cleaned up, but I'd barely slept in my own bed. After three days at Walker's cabin, this place felt cold and empty. I kept listening for Avery's chatter or the sound of Walker moving around the kitchen.

Instead, there was just silence and the memory of what we'd built and destroyed in twelve hours.

For a moment, I let myself sink into the memory of yesterday. "We should talk," he said, when I stepped out of his room the morning after.

My stomach dropped. Nothing good ever started with 'we should talk.'

"Okay," I said carefully.

He ran a hand through his hair, a gesture I was learning meant he was uncomfortable. "Yesterday was... intense."

"It was."

"But I need you to understand something." He finally looked at me, and I saw the walls firmly back in place. "I'm not good at this. At relationships, at letting people in. Rebecca made that pretty clear when she left."

"Walker—"

"I have Avery to think about," he continued, like I hadn't spoken. "She's been through enough upheaval. She doesn't need me bringing someone into her life who's just going to leave again."

The words hit me like a slap. "Who says I'm going to leave?"

"Everyone leaves, Hallie. That's what people do."

The pain in his voice was raw, real, and I wanted to go to him, to smooth away the lines of hurt etched on his face. But something held me back.

"Not everyone," I said quietly.

"No? Then tell me why you're really here. What you're running from."

The question hung between us like a loaded gun. I opened my mouth to deflect, to give him some sanitized version of the truth. Instead, I found myself telling him everything.

"I had a breakdown," I said, the words scraping my throat raw. "Six months ago. Complete mental collapse. I was working sixty-hour weeks at a job I hated, trying to be perfect at everything, and I just... broke."

Walker's expression softened slightly, but he didn't move closer.

"I ended up in the hospital," I continued. "Panic attacks so severe they thought I was having a heart attack. My therapist called it acute anxiety disorder with depressive episodes. Basically, I was so wound up I stopped functioning."

"Hallie—"

"I lost my job. My apartment. My boyfriend decided that crazy wasn't part of his five-year plan and left." I laughed, but it sounded bitter even to my own ears. "So yeah, I'm running. I came here to hide and try to figure out how to be a person again."

The silence that followed was deafening. Walker stared at me with an unreadable expression, and I felt exposed in a way that had nothing to do with nakedness.

"So you see," I said, trying to keep my voice steady, "you're right to be careful. I'm not exactly a good bet."

"That's not what I meant."

"Isn't it?" I clenched his shirt, trying to keep it all together. "You're looking for reasons to push me away because that's easier than taking a risk. And congratulations, I just handed you a perfect one."

"You don't understand—"

"I understand perfectly. You're scared. I get it. I'm scared too. But hiding behind your daughter and your ex-wife's mistakes isn't protecting anyone. It's just making sure you stay lonely."

His jaw tightened. "I'm not lonely."

"No? Then what was yesterday?"

"A mistake," he said, but his voice cracked slightly on the words.

The word hit me square in the chest, even though I'd been expecting it. I nodded carefully, feeling something fragile breaking inside me. I waited a moment longer to see if he would say he didn't mean it, but he stood there silent. I got dressed, packed my things, and left.

I shook the painful memory away, pulled on clothes with shaking hands, and headed downstairs to open the shop, trying to lose myself in the familiar routine of arranging flowers and checking orders. But every time the bell chimed, my heart leaped, hoping it might be him.

It never was.

By noon, I was a wreck. My hands shook as I arranged a funeral spray, and I'd had to remake a wedding bouquet twice because I couldn't concentrate. The carved flower he'd given me sat on my workbench, a beautiful reminder of everything I'd lost.

"You look like hell, honey."

I turned to find Mrs. Patterson in the doorway.

"I'm fine," I lied.

"No, you're not. And neither is that stubborn fool up the mountain." She stepped into the shop, closing the door behind her. "You want to tell me what happened?"

"It's complicated."

"That man is miserable, Hallie. Been holed up in his workshop for three days, working like a demon and snapping at anyone who gets too close. Even Avery's been tiptoeing around him."

My chest tightened at the mention of Avery. I'd grown so attached to that little girl, and now I'd probably never see her again.

"He made his feelings pretty clear," I said quietly. "Called what happened between us a mistake."

"Men say stupid things when they're scared. Doesn't make them true."

"Doesn't make them false either."

Mrs. Patterson studied me with those sharp eyes that saw too much. "You love him."

It wasn't a question, but I answered anyway. "Yeah. I do."

"Then fight for him."

The words hit me square in the chest. "I should get back to work," I said, but my voice lacked conviction.

Mrs. Patterson nodded, but I could see the wheels turning behind her eyes. "You do that, honey. But maybe think about what I said."

She left me standing there with my half-finished arrangements and a heart full of questions I wasn't ready to answer.

## WALKER

I stood in my workshop, staring at the commission piece I'd been working on for three days, and I wanted to put my fist through the wall.

*Mistake.* I'd called what happened between us a mistake.

The look on her face when I'd said it would haunt me for the rest of my life. Like I'd reached into her chest and crushed something vital.

But it was better this way. Safer. She'd told me about her breakdown, her anxiety, and instead of making me want to protect her, it had terrified me. Because I knew what happened when broken people tried to fix each other. I'd learned that people left when things got too hard, when the reality didn't match the fantasy.

Hallie deserved better than another broken person who didn't know how to be what she needed.

She deserved better than me.

I picked up my carving knife and tried to focus on the intricate scrollwork I was creating for a client's mantelpiece. Custom woodworking had been my salvation after my marriage fell apart— something I could control, something that made sense. But even here, in my sanctuary, everything reminded me of her. Her hands learning to carve, her laugh when she got frustrated, the way she'd looked at my work like it mattered.

Like I mattered.

A soft knock on the workshop door made me look up. Avery stood in the doorway, looking uncharacteristically subdued.

"Hey, pumpkin," I said, setting down my tools. "Thought you were playing at Jenny's."

"I was. But I wanted to come home." She stepped into the workshop, her small hands clasped behind her back. "Daddy, are you sad?"

The question hit me like a punch to the gut. "Why would you think that?"

"Because you've been hiding in here for days. And you haven't smiled once since Hallie left." She looked up at me with those serious brown eyes. "I miss her too."

*Miss her too.* Christ. My seven-year-old was handling this better than I was.

"Avery—"

"She made you happy," she said simply. "And you made her happy too. I could tell."

"It's complicated, sweetheart."

"That's what grown-ups always say when they're being stupid." She moved closer, leaning against my workbench. "Mrs. Patterson says you're scared Hallie will leave like Mommy did."

I closed my eyes. Of course Mrs. Patterson had been talking to my daughter about this.

"But Hallie's not like Mommy," Avery continued. "Mommy never helped at the festival. She never made me pancakes or asked about my drawings. And she never looked at you like you were the best thing in the whole world."

The words lodged in my throat. "Avery—"

"I think you should tell her you're sorry," she said with the confidence only children possessed. "And that you want her to come back."

"It's not that simple."

"Why not?"

*Because I'm terrified she'll realize I'm not enough. Because I don't know how to be what she needs. Because losing her now would destroy me.*

"Because sometimes sorry isn't enough," I said finally.

Avery was quiet for a moment, studying me with an expression far too wise for her age. Then she reached into her pocket and pulled out a folded piece of paper.

"I drew this for Hallie," she said, holding it out to me. "Will you give it to her?"

I took the paper with hands that weren't quite steady. It was a drawing of three stick figures standing in front of a cabin—a tall figure with dark hair, a smaller figure with pigtails, and a medium-sized figure with yellow hair. Above them, in Avery's careful printing, were the words: "Our Family."

Something cracked open in my chest.

"She should have it," Avery said. "Even if she can't come back, she should know she's part of our family."

I stared at the drawing, at my daughter's simple, devastating truth, and felt every wall I'd built start to crumble.

Maybe Mrs. Patterson was right. Maybe I was throwing away the best thing that had ever happened to me because I was too scared to take the risk.

Maybe it was time to stop hiding.

The evening brought Mrs. Patterson to my door, holding a covered dish and wearing her concerned grandmother's expression.

"Evening, Walker. Brought you some lasagna."

"Thanks, but I already ate."

She pushed past me into the cabin anyway. "Nonsense. You look like you haven't eaten in days."

I followed her to the kitchen, where she immediately started bustling around, heating up the lasagna and making coffee like she owned the place.

"Heard Hallie's been keeping busy at the shop," she said casually.

My spine stiffened. "Good for her."

"Looked miserable as sin, though. People notice things in a town this small." She fixed me with a look that reminded me why I'd been terrified of her as a kid. "Especially when a perfectly lovely young woman spends her days jumping every time the door chime rings, like she's hoping someone specific might walk through."

"Mrs. Patterson—"

"Don't 'Mrs. Patterson' me, young man. I've known you since you were knee-high to a grasshopper, and I've watched you build walls around yourself ever since you decided that being hurt once meant you should never risk it again. But that girl sees something in you worth fighting for, and you're throwing it away because you're afraid."

"I'm not afraid. I'm being realistic."

"Realistic?" She laughed, but there was no humor in it. "Walker, honey, that girl looked at you like you hung the moon. She defended you to strangers, helped at the festival, fit into your life like she'd always belonged there. And don't get me started on how much Avery adores her—I've never seen your daughter take to someone so fast. You think the realistic thing is to let her go?"

Every word hit home, but I forced myself to stay steady. "She told me about her breakdown. Her anxiety. She needs someone stable, someone who has their shit together."

"And you think you don't?"

"I know I don't."

Mrs. Patterson was quiet for a long moment, studying me with those sharp eyes that saw too much.

"Do you know what I see when I look at you?" she said finally. "I see a man who rebuilt his life from nothing after being abandoned. Who raised a beautiful, confident daughter all by himself.

Who built a successful custom woodworking business from his garage and has never missed a school event or a bedtime story. You think that's not having your shit together?"

"It's not enough."

"For who? Because from where I'm sitting, it looks like more than enough for a woman who just wants someone to love her."

The words lodged in my throat. Love. When had this become about love?

But even as I thought it, I knew the answer. Somewhere between the first time I'd seen her and this morning when I'd woken up in an empty bed, I'd fallen in love with Hallie Blake.

And I'd let her go.

"What if she leaves anyway?" I asked quietly.

"What if she doesn't?" Mrs. Patterson countered. "What if you're throwing away the best thing that's ever happened to you because you're too scared to find out?"

She left the lasagna on the counter when she went, taking only her uncomfortable truths with her. I sat in my empty kitchen, staring at my workshop through the window. I'd been hiding in there for days, throwing myself into commission work, anything to keep my hands busy and my mind off Hallie.

But even my carvings betrayed me. Every piece reminded me of her.

I picked up Avery's drawing from where I'd left it on the counter, staring at the three stick figures she'd labeled "Our Family." My daughter had seen what I'd been too afraid to acknowledge —that Hallie belonged with us.

That we belonged with her.

Maybe love wasn't about being perfect. Maybe it was about being brave enough to show someone your rough edges and trusting them not to cut themselves.

Maybe it was about taking the risk, even when you were terrified.

I stood up abruptly, my mind made up. I was going to find Hallie, and I was going to tell her the truth. That I loved her. That I was sorry. That I wanted to try, if she'd let me.

But first, I had something to carve.

# 7

# THE CARVING BOOTH

**HALLIE**

I was unloading the last of my groceries when Avery appeared.

She materialized like a tiny ninja, wearing her school backpack and a determined expression that reminded me painfully of her father.

"You left," she said. An accusation.

I sank down onto the tailgate, suddenly exhausted. "Yeah, kiddo. It was time to go home."

"Because you got into a fight with Daddy."

Smart kid. Too smart for her own good.

"It's complicated, Avery. I'm just going back to my apartment above the shop. We'll probably see each other around town."

"That's what grown-ups always say but they don't mean it." She marched over and climbed up beside me, swinging her legs. "He's sad, you know."

My chest tightened. "He'll be fine."

"No, he won't. He carved you something new."

I looked at her sharply. "What?"

"Last night. He was in his workshop until really late, and this morning there was wood shavings everywhere." She reached into her backpack and pulled out something wrapped in a school napkin. "He made this for the festival booth, but I think it's really for you."

She unwrapped it carefully, and my breath caught.

It was a sign, carved from dark walnut with letters that looked like they'd been burned into the wood with love. Simple words that hit me like a physical blow:

**"Home is where you're wanted. Stay."**

I stared at it, my vision blurring, and felt something crack open in my chest. This wasn't just wood. This was Walker's heart, carved into something tangible and left for me to find.

"He loves you," Avery said matter-of-factly. "He's just scared you'll leave like Mommy did."

"Avery---"

"But you're not like Mommy. You smell like vanilla and you helped at the festival and you didn't run away when Daddy was grumpy." She fixed me with those serious brown eyes. "You should come back home with us."

"I don't think your dad wants me to come back."

"Then you're not as smart as I thought you were."

Out of the mouths of babes.

I held the sign against my chest, feeling the weight of what Walker had carved into it. Not just the words, but the hope. The fear. The desperate wish that maybe, just maybe, I'd choose to stay.

"Where is he now?" I asked.

"Festival. The carving booth." Avery grinned, gap-toothed and victorious. "You should hurry. The contest ends at five."

I looked at the little girl who'd somehow become my champion, this fierce creature who'd decided her grumpy father needed someone to love him. "What if he doesn't want to see me?"

"Then he wouldn't have carved you a sign."

Simple logic. Devastating truth.

I hugged her quickly, breathing in the scent of apple juice and determination. "Thank you."

"You're welcome. Now go get him before someone else does."

The festival was winding down when I arrived, families packing up their pumpkins and sticky-faced children dragging tired parents toward the parking lot. I found the carving booth easily enough---it was the one surrounded by a small crowd of people admiring the demonstrations.

And there was Walker, exactly where Avery had said he'd be.

He was helping a young boy carve a simple pumpkin, his big hands guiding small fingers with infinite patience. He looked tired, I noticed. Hollow around the eyes like he hadn't slept. But he was smiling at the kid, encouraging him when the carving went crooked.

"That's it," he said. "Don't worry about making it perfect. Sometimes the best things are a little rough around the edges."

The irony wasn't lost on me.

I stood at the edge of the crowd, clutching his sign and trying to work up the courage to approach. What if he really didn't want me back? What if yesterday had been just sex for him, and I was about to make a fool of myself in front of half the town?

But then his gaze found mine across the crowd, and everything else fell away.

He went perfectly still, his hands freezing mid-motion. The boy he was helping looked up at him in confusion, but Walker didn't notice. He was staring at me like I was an apparition, like he couldn't quite believe I was real.

I held up the sign, and something raw and desperate flashed across his face.

The crowd seemed to sense the shift in energy. Conversations died down, heads turned, and suddenly I was the center of attention in a way that would normally have sent me running.

Instead, I walked toward him.

"You carved me something," I said when I was close enough that he could hear me.

"I carved you a lot of things," he said roughly. "Most of them I was too much of a coward to give you."

"This one says to stay."

"It does."

"Is that what you want? For me to stay?"

The silence stretched between us, loaded with everything we'd said and hadn't said, everything we'd broken and might still be able to fix.

"Yes," he said finally, his voice carrying across the booth. "I want you to stay. I want to try this thing between us, even though I'll probably fuck it up. Even though I'm scared as hell. Even though I don't deserve you."

"You don't get to decide what you deserve," I said, stepping closer. "I do. And I think you deserve someone who sees all your rough edges and chooses to stay anyway."

"Hallie---"

"I love you," I said, cutting him off. "I love your grumpy morning voice and the way you encourage Avery to be her true self. I love that you carve beautiful things with your hands and that you'd rather chop wood than make small talk. I love that you're scared and brave at the same time."

The crowd around us had gone completely quiet, but I didn't care. This was too important for embarrassment.

"I had a breakdown," I continued. "I might have another one.

I'm anxious and broken, and I don't know what I'm doing half the time. But I know I want to do it with you, if you'll let me."

Walker's eyes were bright, too bright, and when he spoke his voice was rough with emotion. "I love you too. So much it terrifies me."

He came around the table then, moving toward me with purpose, and I met him halfway. When his arms came around me, lifting me off my feet, the crowd erupted in cheers and applause.

"Stay," he whispered against my ear. "Please stay."

"I'm not going anywhere," I whispered back. "Home is where you're wanted, right?"

He pulled back to look at me, his dark eyes soft with love and relief and something that looked like forever. "Right here. You're wanted right here."

He kissed me then, deep and thorough and completely uncaring of our audience. I melted into him, tasting coffee and promises and the future we were brave enough to build together.

When we finally broke apart, I found Avery at the edge of the crowd, grinning like she'd personally orchestrated world peace.

"Told you so," she called out, and the crowd laughed.


**WALKER**

Three months later, I woke up to the smell of coffee and the sound of Hallie singing in my kitchen.

*My* kitchen. *My* woman. *My* life had somehow become everything I'd never known I wanted.

She was wearing one of my flannel shirts and nothing else, dancing barefoot while she made breakfast. Her hair was a mess, there was flour on her cheek, and she was completely, utterly perfect.

"Morning," I said from the doorway.

She spun around, beaming at me. "Morning. I made pancakes. Christmas tree-shaped, obviously."

"Obviously." I crossed to her, pulling her into my arms and breathing in the scent of vanilla and home. "Very festive for December. Sleep okay?"

"Better than okay." She stood on her toes to kiss me. "You?"

"Best night's sleep of my life," I said, which was true. Every night with her was the best night of my life.

We'd taken it slow after the festival. Dates, conversations, careful steps toward something that felt like forever. She'd moved back into her little apartment once it was fixed up, but most nights she ended up here. Most mornings I woke up with her in my arms.

It was perfect. We were perfect.

Well, mostly perfect. There were still moments when the fear crept in, when I worried I'd mess this up or she'd realize she deserved better. But Hallie had a way of chasing away the darkness with her laughter and her terrible jokes and her absolute certainty that we belonged together.

"Daddy! Hallie!" Avery's voice carried from the loft. "Can we have hot chocolate with breakfast?"

"It's eight o'clock in the morning," I called back.

"So? It's still winter!"

Hallie grinned. "Hot chocolate it is."

This was my life now. Mornings filled with laughter and pancakes and the two most important people in my world. I'd never imagined it could be this good.

"Hey," Hallie said softly, running her hands up my chest. "You okay? You look thoughtful."

"Just thinking about how lucky I am."

"We both are." She kissed me again, soft and sweet. "I love you, Walker Boone."

"I love you too."

And I did. Completely, desperately, forever.

The sound of a truck pulling up outside made us both look toward the window. Through the glass, I could see Lynx climbing out of his beat-up Ford, looking uncharacteristically nervous.

"Wonder what that's about," Hallie murmured.

I had a pretty good idea. Lynx had been acting strange lately---distracted, jumpy, asking weird questions about women and relationships. Either he was having some kind of crisis, or he'd met someone.

Given the way he kept checking his phone and the fact that he'd actually combed his hair, I was betting on the latter.

"Probably needs to borrow tools," I said, but I was grinning. If Lynx had finally found someone brave enough to handle him, this was going to be interesting.

The knock on the door was followed immediately by Avery thundering down the stairs.

"I'll get it!" she announced, then paused to beam at Hallie and me. "You two look happy."

"We are happy," Hallie said, and the simple truth of it hit me square in the chest.

We were happy. Finally, completely, ridiculously happy.

And as I watched my daughter open the door to whatever adventure was coming next, with the woman I loved warm in my arms, I couldn't imagine wanting anything more than this.

This messy, imperfect, absolutely perfect life we'd carved out together.

THE END

# BRANDED
# MOUNTAIN MAN

# 1

## THE TOWER

SLOAN

The trail to the old fire tower was supposed to be a quick hike. In and out. Check on the isolated trail worker, confirm he was still breathing and hadn't gone completely feral, file a report, and head back to civilization.

That was the plan, anyway.

Now, two hours into what should have been a forty-five-minute climb, Sloan Whitaker was beginning to suspect the Forest Service had sent her on a wild goose chase. The GPS coordinates led to nothing but overgrown switchbacks and what appeared to be an abandoned trail marker from the Clinton administration.

"Brilliant," she muttered, adjusting her pack and glaring at her phone. No signal. Of course. "Send the wilderness therapist to check on the hermit. What could go wrong?"

She'd volunteered for this pilot program because it made sense —trail workers spent months alone in the backcountry, and mental health support was practically nonexistent. Someone needed to make sure they weren't slowly losing their minds to isolation and pine trees.

She just hadn't expected to lose her own mind trying to find them.

The trail curved sharply ahead, and Sloan pushed through a tangle of overgrown ferns before stopping dead.

There it was. The fire tower.

Or what was left of it.

The structure rose sixty feet into the sky, its metal framework intact but clearly abandoned for years. Except it wasn't abandoned now. Fresh lumber was stacked in neat piles around the base. A generator hummed quietly in the distance. And someone had been busy—the stairs were rebuilt, the platform reinforced, and the cab at the top looked like it might actually keep the weather out.

Movement caught her eye. A man emerged from behind the tower, carrying an armload of lumber like it weighed nothing. Tall, broad-shouldered, and wearing a flannel shirt that had seen better decades. Someone who knew mountains, who belonged in wild spaces.

He spotted her at the same moment she spotted him.

And he did not look happy.

"You lost?" His voice carried across the clearing, rough and unwelcoming.

Sloan squared her shoulders and walked closer. "Colt Ramsey?"

He set down the lumber with deliberate care and straightened. Up close, he was even more imposing. Early forties, she guessed, with dark hair that needed a cut and a beard that needed trimming. His hands were scarred and calloused, his jeans torn at the knee, and he looked at her like she was trespassing.

Which, technically, she probably was.

"Depends who's asking." His eyes were the color of storm clouds, and just as welcoming.

"Sloan Whitaker. Forest Service sent me."

Something shifted in his expression. Surprise, then irritation. "They sent you to check on me?"

"That's the idea." She kept her voice level, professional. "New pilot program. Mental health wellness checks for isolated trail workers."

He stared at her for a long moment, then turned and picked up his lumber again. "I'm fine. You can leave now."

Sloan blinked. "I'm sorry?"

"You heard me." He started walking toward the tower. "Thanks for the visit. Don't get lost on your way down."

"I'm not leaving." The words came out sharper than she'd intended. "I hiked two hours to get here, and I have a job to do."

Colt stopped walking and slowly turned around. "Your job was to check if I'm still alive. I'm alive. Job done."

"That's not how this works—"

"This is how it works." He stepped closer, and Sloan had to tilt her head back to maintain eye contact. "I didn't ask for a babysitter. I don't need a therapist. And I sure as hell don't need some city girl hiking up here to tell me how to feel about my life."

City girl. Sloan's temper flared. "I'm from Montana, actually. And I've spent more time in the wilderness than most of your trail crew combined."

"Good for you." He turned away again. "Use all that wilderness experience to find your way back down the mountain."

A low rumble of thunder rolled across the valley, and Sloan glanced up at the sky. The afternoon clouds had been building while she'd been focused on finding the tower, and they'd gone from puffy white to ominous gray while she wasn't paying attention.

"Shit." She pulled out her phone to check the weather app, but still, there was no signal.

"Storm's moving fast." Colt's voice had lost some of its hostility, replaced by something that sounded almost like concern. "You need to get down the mountain. Now."

Another rumble, closer this time. The wind picked up, sending pine needles skittering across the clearing.

Sloan looked at the trail she'd just climbed, then at the darkening sky. She was a competent hiker, but she wasn't stupid. Getting caught in a mountain storm was a cautionary tale in itself.

"How long until it hits?"

Colt glanced at the clouds, his expression grim. "Twenty minutes. Maybe less."

The first fat raindrops splattered against her cheek as if to prove his point.

"Fuck." Sloan ran a hand through her hair, weighing her options. They were all bad. "Okay. I need shelter."

"Tower's the only option." He didn't sound happy about it, but he was already moving toward the stairs. "Come on. Before this gets ugly."

She followed him up the newly rebuilt steps, her pack bouncing against her back as the wind picked up. By the time they reached the platform, the rain was coming down in earnest.

Colt yanked open the door to the cab and gestured her inside. "Welcome to the Ritz."

The interior of the fire tower was small but functional. Someone—Colt, obviously—had turned it into a livable space. A narrow cot was pushed against one wall, with a small wood stove opposite and a tiny table that served as both a desk and a kitchen counter. Everything was clean, organized, and utterly masculine.

"You live here?" Sloan asked, setting down her pack.

"I work here." He moved around the small space with familiar efficiency, checking the windows and adjusting something on the stove. "Storm should blow through by morning."

Morning. Sloan processed that information with growing unease. "I can't stay overnight. All of my belongings are at base camp. I was only supposed to come up to do an introduction before we did some hiking tomorrow."

"You can't leave, either." Colt pulled off his flannel and hung it on a peg by the door, leaving him in a faded gray t-shirt that clung to his chest and shoulders. "Unless you want me to explain to the Forest Service why their therapist died of exposure on her first wellness check."

Outside, the wind howled, and rain lashed against the windows. Lightning flickered, followed by a crack of thunder that made the whole tower vibrate.

Sloan looked around the tiny space, then at Colt, who was watching her with an expression she couldn't quite read.

"This is going to be a long night," she said.

"Yeah." His voice was rough, quiet. "It is."

## COLT

Colt Ramsey had been living alone on this mountain for years now, and he'd gotten good at avoiding people. He'd chosen this place specifically because it was off the beaten path, forgotten, and far enough from civilization that unexpected visitors were impossible.

Apparently, he hadn't gone far enough.

The woman—Sloan—stood in the middle of his carefully organized space like she belonged there, dripping rainwater onto his floor and looking around with the kind of professional assessment that made his teeth itch. She was exactly what he'd expected from the Forest Service: competent, confident, and completely out of place.

She was also nothing like what he'd expected.

For one thing, she was curvy in all the right places, with long, dark hair that was escaping from her ponytail and brown eyes that seemed to see too much. For another, she hadn't backed down when he'd tried to intimidate her into leaving. Most people took one look at him and decided they had somewhere else to be.

Not Sloan Whitaker.

She shrugged out of her rain jacket and hung it next to his flannel, the movement pulling her t-shirt tight across her chest. Colt forced himself to look away and busied himself with stoking the fire.

"So," she said, settling onto the single chair at his table. "How long have you been up here?"

"Long enough."

"That's not an answer."

Colt glanced at her, irritated. "Three years."

"Three years." She repeated it like she was filing it away for later analysis. "And before that?"

"Before that doesn't matter."

"It might—"

"No." The word came out harder than he'd intended, and Sloan went quiet. Good. Maybe she'd get the message.

Outside, the storm was intensifying. Rain drummed against the roof, and the wind made the tower sway just enough to remind them they were sixty feet off the ground. Colt had been through dozens of storms up here, but never with company.

Never with a woman who smelled like vanilla and rain and looked at him like she was trying to solve a puzzle.

He glanced at her again, taking in the way she sat with perfect posture despite the uncomfortable chair, the way her eyes tracked his movements around the small space. She was cataloging him, he realized. Making mental notes for whatever report she'd file when she got back to town.

The thought made his jaw clench.

"You're not what I expected," Sloan said suddenly.

"What did you expect?"

"Someone more..." She gestured vaguely. "Feral, I guess. Living off squirrels and talking to trees."

Despite himself, Colt's mouth almost twitched. "I eat canned food like a civilized person. And the trees are terrible conversationalists."

Was that almost a smile on her face? It was gone too quickly for him to be sure.

"The tower looks good," she said, looking around again. "You've done a lot of work up here."

"Needed something to do."

"Most people find other things to do when they're bored. Hobbies. Netflix."

"Most people don't live sixty feet off the ground with no internet."

"Most people don't choose to live sixty feet off the ground with no internet."

There it was again—that assessing look. Like she was trying to figure out what was wrong with him. Colt turned back to the fire, feeding it another piece of wood and watching the flames dance.

"Why did you?" she asked quietly.

"Why did I what?"

"Choose this."

The question hung in the air between them, weighted with implications he didn't want to explore. Outside, lightning flashed, illuminating the rain-soaked windows for a split second before thunder followed.

"Because it's quiet," he said finally.

"Quiet can be good." Her voice was gentler now, less professional. "It can also be isolating."

"That's the point."

"Is it?"

Colt turned to look at her, ready with a sharp response, but something in her expression stopped him. She wasn't judging him. She wasn't taking notes for her report. She was just... watching him. Waiting.

"I don't need fixing," he said instead.

"I didn't say you did."

"That's why you're here, isn't it? To fix the broken mountain man?"

Sloan was quiet for a moment, considering. "I'm here to make sure you're okay. There's a difference."

"I'm fine."

"Are you?"

The simple question hit harder than it should have. Colt felt something twist in his chest, a familiar ache he'd gotten good at ignoring. He was fine. He'd been fine for three years. He'd keep being fine as long as people left him alone.

"I'm fine," he repeated, more firmly this time.

"Okay." Sloan nodded, but her eyes stayed on his face. "Then we'll just wait out the storm."

She pulled a paperback book from her pack and settled back in the chair, apparently content to read while the weather raged outside. Colt watched her for a moment, nonplussed. He'd expected more questions, more probing, more of the therapeutic bulldozing he'd been dreading.

Instead, she was giving him space.

He didn't know what to do with that.

The storm intensified, shaking the tower and sending sheets of rain against the windows. It was going to be a long night, trapped in this small space with a woman who made him hyperaware of things he'd forgotten about. The way she moved. The sound of her breathing. The fact that he hadn't been this close to another person in months.

Colt settled onto his cot and tried to focus on anything other than the curve of her hip or the way she bit her lower lip when she was concentrating on her book.

This was going to be a very long night.

# 2

## MAN OF FEW WORDS

**COLT**

Colt woke to the sound of someone moving around his space, and for a split second, muscle memory kicked in. His hand was halfway to the knife under his pillow before his brain caught up.

Sloan. The therapist. The storm.

Right.

He lay still on the narrow cot, watching through half-closed eyes as she quietly rearranged items on his makeshift counter. She'd been up for a while, judging by the fresh cup of coffee steaming next to his untouched first aid kit—which she was now examining with obvious disapproval.

"Expired aspirin and butterfly bandages," she murmured to herself, checking dates on pill bottles. "Jesus Christ, when did you last restock this thing?"

"It's fine," Colt said, his voice rougher than he'd intended.

Sloan jumped, nearly dropping the bottle in her hand. "You're awake."

"Hard to sleep when someone's ransacking my stuff."

"I'm not ransacking. I'm organizing." She held up a bottle of painkillers that were probably older than her hiking boots. "These expired two years ago."

"They still work."

"That's not how medication works." She set the bottle aside with the kind of deliberate care that suggested she was trying not to throw it out the window. "When did you last see a doctor?"

Colt sat up slowly, his left leg protesting the movement. The old injury always acted up in bad weather, and last night's storm had his knee feeling like broken glass. "Don't need a doctor."

"Everyone needs a doctor sometimes." Her eyes tracked the way he favored his left side as he stood, and he could practically see her making mental notes. "How long have you been limping?"

"I'm not limping."

"Right. And I'm not a therapist." She poured herself more coffee from the pot on his camp stove, completely at home in his space. "Want some?"

Colt wanted to say no. Wanted to maintain the distance, the walls, the careful isolation he'd built around himself. Instead, he found himself nodding.

She handed him a mug, and their fingers brushed for a split second. Her skin was warm, soft, completely unlike his own scarred hands. She noticed the contrast too—he saw her glance down at the contact before quickly looking away.

The coffee mug slipped from her fingers as Colt's eyes went dark, his gaze dropping to where his flannel gaped open across her chest.

"Sloan." Her name sounded rough, desperate.

"I know we shouldn't—"

"We definitely shouldn't." But his thumb traced her lower lip anyway, and when she bit down gently, he groaned. "This is such a bad idea."

"The worst," she agreed, then pulled him down for a kiss that tasted like bad decisions and perfect timing.

"Storm's still moving through," she said, gesturing toward the windows. Outside, the rain continued to drum against the glass, though not as violently as the night before. "But there's another system behind it. Weather service is calling for three days of intermittent storms."

Three days. Colt felt something twist in his chest—part dread, part anticipation. "You can't stay here for three days."

"I don't have much choice. My assignment is for 72 hours anyway—standard protocol for psychological wellness assessments. The storms just mean we're doing it here instead of me hiking back and forth."

"Seventy-two hours." The words came out flat.

"Three days to observe, assess, and determine if you need additional support services." She settled back into the chair with her coffee, studying his face. "Don't look so thrilled."

Colt turned away, busying himself with stoking the fire. Three days trapped in this small space with a woman who made him hyperaware of things he'd forgotten about. The way she moved. The sound of her breathing. The fact that he hadn't been this close to another person in months.

"You don't have to be an asshole about it, you know," she said quietly. "I'm not here to judge you."

"Aren't you?"

"No." She met his eyes over her coffee mug. "I'm here because isolation can mess with people's heads. Make them think they're fine when they're not. Make them push away help when they need it most."

"I don't need help."

"Everyone needs help sometimes."

"You said that already."

"Because it's true." She leaned forward slightly, and Colt caught another hint of that vanilla scent that had been driving him crazy all night. "How long since you've talked to another person? Before yesterday, I mean."

Colt thought about it. Nash had hiked up about six weeks ago, bringing supplies and checking on the tower's progress. Before that... "Couple of months."

"Don't you get lonely?"

The question hit something deep in his chest, a place he'd learned to keep locked down tight. Lonely didn't begin to cover it. But lonely was better than the alternative. Lonely was safer than letting people close enough to leave.

"I like the quiet," he said instead.

"Quiet's not the same as isolation."

"It is for me."

Sloan studied his face, and Colt had the uncomfortable feeling she was seeing more than he wanted her to. "What happened to your leg?"

"Accident."

"What kind of accident?"

"The kind that's none of your business."

She didn't flinch at the edge in his voice. If anything, she leaned back in her chair and got more comfortable, like she was settling in for a long conversation. "You know what I think?"

"I'm sure you're going to tell me."

"I think you're scared."

Colt went very still. "Excuse me?"

"I think you're up here hiding because you're scared of what happens if you let people get close. And I think you're in pain—physical pain—and you're too stubborn to do anything about it because taking care of yourself would mean admitting you're human."

Heat flared in his chest, sharp and familiar. "You don't know anything about me."

"I know you've been living alone for three years with expired medication and a limp you won't acknowledge. I know you built this place into something beautiful, but you won't let anyone see it. And I know you're hurting—not just physically."

"You're wrong."

"Am I?"

Colt set down his coffee mug with deliberate control, fighting the urge to throw it against the wall. "You've been here twelve hours. You don't get to psychoanalyze my life."

"I'm not psychoanalyzing. I'm observing."

"Same thing."

"Not even close." She stood up, and suddenly the small space felt even smaller. "Psychoanalyzing would be me telling you why you're hiding. Observing is me noticing that you are."

"The storm's clearing. You should go."

"Should I? Because I'm pretty sure I just told you I'm here for three days." She moved toward the window, checking the conditions outside. "And looking at those clouds, I'd say we're in for another round tonight."

She was right, damn her. The sky was still heavy with moisture, and the wind hadn't died down the way it should have if the system was truly moving through.

"Besides," she added, turning back to him with a slight smile, "I'm curious about your work up here. The tower restoration, the trail maintenance. You've done incredible work. Mind showing me around?"

## SLOAN

Sloan had been watching Colt Ramsey for eighteen hours now, and she was starting to understand that her standard assessment techniques weren't going to work with him.

He was too guarded, too practiced at deflecting questions. Too used to being alone with his thoughts.

What she needed was to see him in action. See how he moved through his world, what brought him comfort, what made him come alive.

"You want to see the tower?" Colt asked, suspicion clear in his voice.

"I want to understand what you've built here. What keeps you grounded." She gestured toward the windows, where morning light was filtering through the clouds. "Call it wilderness therapy if you want. Sometimes the best way to understand someone is to see them in their element."

"This isn't therapy."

"No. It's just two people spending time together." She pulled on her boots, checking the laces. "Unless you'd rather sit in here and glare at each other for the next three days."

Something shifted in his expression—surprise, maybe, or reluctant interest. "You're not what I expected from a therapist."

"What did you expect?"

"Someone more..." He gestured vaguely. "Clinical. Someone who'd want to sit and talk about feelings."

"Feelings are important. But sometimes they're easier to access when your hands are busy and your mind isn't so focused on defending itself."

Colt was quiet for a moment, considering. Then he moved toward the door. "Fine. But we do this my way. You follow my lead, stay where I tell you to stay, and don't touch anything without asking."

"Deal."

The next few hours were a revelation.

Outside the small confines of the tower cab, Colt transformed. His movements became sure and economical as he showed her the rebuilt stairs, the reinforced platform, the careful attention to detail in every joint and connection.

"The original structure was built in the fifties," he explained, running his hand along a support beam. "Good bones, but decades of weather had taken their toll. When I got here, half the stairs were rotted through and the cab was basically a sieve."

"You did all this yourself?"

"Mostly. Nash brought materials when he could—good man, the kind who doesn't abandon his people—but yeah."

Sloan watched him work as he demonstrated the restoration techniques he'd used, noting the way his shoulders relaxed when he was focused on a task. The care in his hands as he adjusted a loose board. The pride he tried to hide when she complimented his craftsmanship.

"It's beautiful work," she said, meaning it. "You should be proud of what you've accomplished."

"It's just maintenance."

"No, it's not. This is art. Functional art, but art nonetheless."

Colt glanced at her, something flickering in his expression that looked almost like gratitude. "Marcus would have liked it. He was always on me about taking pride in the work."

It was the first time he'd mentioned anyone from his past without prompting. Sloan filed the name away, but didn't push. Instead, she followed him as he led her around the perimeter of the tower, pointing out drainage improvements and erosion control measures.

"You've been busy," she observed.

"Had time to kill."

"This is more than killing time. This is someone building something to last. Something that matters."

Colt stopped walking and turned to look at her. "Why are you really here, Sloan?"

The question caught her off guard with its directness. "What do you mean?"

"I mean, you could have done your assessment yesterday. Asked your questions, made your notes, hiked out this morning and filed whatever report you're going to file. But you're still here. Why?"

Sloan considered her answer carefully. The professional response would be to mention her 72-hour protocol, her need for thorough documentation. But standing here with Colt in the clean mountain air, watching him be fully present for the first time since she'd arrived, she found herself wanting to be honest.

"Because I think you're worth the time," she said simply.

The words hung in the air between them, loaded with implications neither of them was ready to examine. Colt's face went carefully blank, but she saw the way his hands clenched at his sides.

"You don't know me."

"No. But I know you built something beautiful up here. I know you've been taking care of yourself, even if you won't admit it. And I know there's more to your story than you're telling me."

"Everyone has stories."

"True. But not everyone isolates themselves for three years because of them."

Thunder rolled across the valley, and they both looked up at the darkening sky. The next storm was building faster than expected.

"We should head back," Colt said.

As they climbed the stairs to the tower, Sloan felt a shift between them. The hostility from the morning had mellowed into something more complex—part wariness, part curiosity, part recognition of something that might become understanding given time.

Three days suddenly didn't seem like nearly enough.

# 3

## THE BRAND

**SLOAN**

By the second day, Sloan had fallen into a rhythm with Colt that felt dangerously natural.

She'd wake to coffee already brewing—he was up first, moving around the small space with careful quiet. They ate breakfast while checking the weather, then spent the morning working together on whatever project he'd planned for the day.

Today it was trail maintenance down the ridge, repairing washouts from the recent storms. Sloan had offered to help after watching him struggle with a particularly stubborn drainage channel, and to her surprise, he'd accepted.

"Hand me that shovel," Colt said, not looking up from where he was digging out debris.

Sloan passed it over, then moved to the other side of the washout to start clearing from that end. They'd been working in comfortable silence for an hour, and she could see the tension in his shoulders easing as he focused on the physical work.

This was what she'd hoped for when she'd suggested the wilderness therapy approach. Colt was more open when his hands were busy, less guarded when he wasn't being directly questioned. She'd learned more about him in the past day of working alongside him than she would have in weeks of traditional sessions.

"You're good at this," she said, nodding toward the neat way he'd rerouted the water flow around a boulder.

"Had plenty of practice."

"Before the tower, you mean?"

Colt's movements stilled slightly. "Yeah. Before."

Sloan waited, not pushing, just continuing to work. She'd learned that silence was often more effective than questions with him.

"Worked trail crew for eight years," he said finally. "After the military. Good work. Honest work."

"What made you stop?"

The question hung in the air between them, and Sloan immediately regretted asking it. Too direct. Too much like therapy.

Colt straightened up, his expression closing off. "Doesn't matter."

"I'm sorry. I didn't mean to pry."

"Yes, you did." He set down his tools and turned to face her fully. "That's what this is, isn't it? All of this. The working together, the casual questions, the way you act like we're just two people spending time together. It's all just therapy."

Heat flared in Sloan's chest. "That's not—"

"Isn't it?" Colt stepped closer, and she could see anger building in his storm-gray eyes. "You're studying me. Taking mental notes. Figuring out what's broken so you can write it up in your report."

"I'm trying to understand you."

"Why? So you can fix me?"

"Because I care about you." The words slipped out before she could stop them, raw and honest and completely unprofessional.

Colt stared at her for a moment, something shifting in his expression. Then his face hardened again. "No, you don't. You care about doing your job. About being the therapist who cracked the tough case."

"That's not true."

"Prove it."

"How?"

"Stop analyzing me. Stop trying to get me to open up. Stop pretending this is anything other than what it is—you doing your job."

Sloan felt something crack inside her chest. "And what if I can't? What if this stopped being just a job somewhere between you making me coffee and showing me how you rebuilt those stairs?"

The honesty in her voice seemed to catch Colt off guard. His anger faltered, replaced by something that looked almost like vulnerability.

"Then you're making a mistake," he said quietly.

"Maybe. But it's my mistake to make."

They stared at each other across the small space, the air thick with tension and unspoken truths. Thunder rumbled in the distance, and Sloan glanced up at the sky. Another storm was building—the third in as many days.

"We should head back," Colt said, but he didn't move.

"Colt—"

"Don't." He held up a hand, stepping away from her. "Whatever you're about to say, don't. Because if you're right, if this isn't just therapy for you, then we have a problem."

"What kind of problem?"

"The kind where people get hurt."

Before Sloan could respond, the first fat raindrops began to fall. Within minutes, it was coming down hard enough to make the trail treacherous.

They made it back to the tower just as the storm hit in earnest, both of them soaked and breathing hard from the climb. But the physical distance between them felt like nothing compared to the emotional chasm that had opened up.

"I need to change," Sloan said, grabbing dry clothes from her pack.

"Yeah." Colt moved to the window, presenting his back to her. "Me too."

As Sloan peeled off her wet shirt, she caught sight of Colt's reflection in the glass. He was watching her, his expression unguarded for just a moment, and the raw want in his eyes made her breath catch.

Then he noticed her looking and turned away abruptly.

"This isn't working," he said, his voice rough.

"What isn't working?"

"This. Us. Whatever this is." He pulled off his own wet shirt, and Sloan saw the scar tissue covering his left side. But this time, instead of looking away, she studied it openly.

"Someone branded you," she said quietly.

Colt went very still. "It's not what you think."

"Then tell me what it is."

"It's mine to carry."

"I know. But you don't have to carry it alone."

"Yes, I do." He turned to face her, and the expression on his face was raw, desperate. "Because everyone I let close gets hurt. Everyone I care about pays the price for my mistakes."

"What mistakes?"

"I killed my best friend."

The words hung in the air between them like a physical blow.

Sloan felt her chest tighten, not with shock, but with understanding. This was it—the wound he'd been protecting, the guilt that had driven him to this mountain.

"Tell me," she said softly.

## COLT

The story came out in broken pieces, like shards of glass that cut him as he spoke.

Marcus. The fire. The choice that had killed the best man he'd ever known.

He told her about the brand—how it had started as military survival training, meant to teach them what capture and torture felt like. How after Marcus died, the symbol had become something else entirely. A reminder. A punishment he'd given himself by trying to burn it away.

"The fire that damaged it came later," he said, his voice barely above a whisper. "Second year up here. I was drinking, feeling sorry for myself, and I decided the brand wasn't enough punishment. Decided I needed to finish what I started."

Sloan's face had gone very still, very quiet. "You tried to burn it off."

"Tried to burn it all off." He could still remember that night, the desperate grief that had driven him to hold his own skin to the flames. "Marcus pulled me out of the fire the day he died. Seemed fitting that fire should be what finished me."

"But you stopped."

"Marcus stopped me." The admission came out broken, barely audible. "I heard his voice. Clear as day, telling me to stop being a fucking idiot. So I did."

For a long moment, neither of them spoke. Outside, the storm raged against the windows, but inside the tower, everything was still.

"That's why you're up here," Sloan said finally. "You're punishing yourself."

"I'm keeping myself where I can't hurt anyone else."

"That's not the same thing."

"Isn't it?"

She moved closer, and Colt had to fight the urge to back away. "You made a bad call in an impossible situation. That doesn't make you a killer."

"It makes me responsible."

"It makes you human."

"Don't." The word tore out of him, raw and desperate. "Don't you get it? Everyone I care about gets hurt. Everyone I touch gets burned. Marcus is dead because I was careless."

"And you think if you care about me, I'll get hurt too."

"I know you will."

Sloan was quiet for a long moment, studying his face. When she spoke, her voice was steady, certain.

"That's the biggest load of bullshit I've ever heard."

Colt blinked. "What?"

"You heard me. It's bullshit, Colt. Self-indulgent, narcissistic bullshit."

Anger flared in his chest, hot and familiar. "You don't know what you're talking about."

"Don't I? You're so busy playing the tragic hero that you can't see how insulting this is."

"Insulting?"

"To Marcus. To his memory. To me." Sloan's eyes were blazing now, all professional composure forgotten. "You think Marcus would want this? Want you hiding up here, punishing yourself for the rest of your life?"

"He's dead. What he wants doesn't matter."

"It's the only thing that matters." She moved closer, and despite himself, Colt found his hand moving instinctively to cover the brand beneath his shirt. "You're using his death as an excuse to avoid living. You're dishonoring everything he died for."

The words hit him like a physical blow. Colt felt something crack open in his chest, three years of carefully controlled grief threatening to spill out.

"He died for nothing," he said quietly.

"He died for you. And you're throwing that gift away."

"It wasn't a gift."

"Then what was it?"

Colt stared at her, this woman who'd walked into his carefully constructed exile and torn it apart in two days. Who'd touched his scars like they were beautiful and called him on his bullshit when no one else would.

"I don't know," he admitted.

"Then maybe it's time to figure it out."

The storm outside intensified, shaking the tower and sending sheets of rain against the windows. But inside, something had shifted between them. The careful distance Sloan had been maintaining was gone, replaced by something rawer, more honest.

More dangerous.

"Why do you care?" Colt asked quietly. "You don't know me."

"I know enough." She reached out slowly, giving him time to pull away, and placed her hand flat against his chest where the brand lay hidden beneath his shirt. "I know you're a good man who's been hurt. I know you've been carrying guilt that isn't yours to carry. And I know that whatever happened to Marcus, it wasn't your fault."

"You don't understand—"

"Then help me understand."

The simple request broke something loose inside him. Without fully realizing what he was doing, Colt found himself pulling off his shirt, exposing the twisted mass of scar tissue that covered his left side.

In the firelight, the brand was clearly visible—a deliberate pattern burned deep into his flesh, then torn through by the fire that had nearly killed him. It was ugly, brutal, a map of his failures carved into his skin.

But when Sloan looked at it, there was no revulsion in her eyes. No pity. Just a deep, quiet acceptance that made his chest tight with something he couldn't name.

"It's not ugly," she said softly, her fingers tracing the raised edges of the scarring. "It's survival."

And for the first time in three years, Colt began to believe that might be true.

The radio crackled to life, Nash's familiar voice cutting through the static. "Tower Four, you copy?"

Colt moved to the radio, jaw tight. "Copy."

"Weather clearing your way? Heard that system was a beast."

"We're fine." Colt's response was clipped, professional.

"We?"

A pause. Colt glanced at Sloan, who was pretending not to listen. "Assessment's still in progress."

"Copy that. Check in tomorrow, yeah?"

"Yeah."

When he clicked off, Sloan was watching him. "He cares about you."

"He's just doing his job."

"No. That wasn't his job voice. That was his friend voice."

Colt said nothing, but something in his expression softened.

# 4

## THE FIRE INSIDE

COLT

Colt had forgotten what it felt like to want something this badly.

Two days of careful distance, two days of watching Sloan move through his space like she belonged there, and it all crumbled the moment her hand touched his scarred skin. She looked at his brand—his shame, his failure—like it was something sacred instead of something hideous.

She kissed him like she was starving, like she'd been waiting for this as long as he had, and the sound she made when his tongue touched hers sent fire straight through his veins.

"Wait," he managed, pulling back just enough to see her face. "You don't know what you're doing."

"I know exactly what I'm doing." Her hands were already working at the button of his jeans, sure and deliberate. "Do you?"

Did he? Colt couldn't think past the feel of her fingers against his skin, the way she looked in his flannel shirt with her hair messed and her lips swollen from his kiss. She was so fucking beautiful it hurt to look at her.

"This isn't—" He tried to find the words, tried to hold onto some thread of sanity. "I'm not good for you."

"I don't care."

"You should."

"Maybe." She pushed his jeans down his hips, her touch confident and unashamed. "But I don't."

When her hand wrapped around him, Colt's vision went white. He'd been hard since the moment she'd touched his scar, but her skin on his was something else entirely. Electric. Devastating.

"Fuck," he breathed, his hips jerking forward involuntarily.

"That's the idea." Sloan's voice was rough with want, and when he looked down at her, her eyes were dark with the same desperate need clawing at his chest.

He should have been gentle. Should have taken his time, made sure she was ready, treated her like the precious thing she was. Instead, he yanked the flannel shirt over her head and pinned her beneath him on the narrow cot, his mouth finding the sensitive spot where her neck met her shoulder.

She arched under him, her nails digging into his back hard enough to leave marks. "More."

"You're sure?" Even as he asked, his hands were mapping her curves, learning the shape of her like he was memorizing it for the long winter ahead.

"God, yes." She wrapped her legs around his waist, pulling him closer. "I'm sure."

Colt buried his face against her throat and let himself fall.

There was nothing careful about the way he took her. Nothing controlled or measured or sane. She met him thrust for thrust, her body rising to his like she'd been made for this, made for him, and when she came apart in his arms the first time, he had to bite down on his own tongue to keep from saying something stupid.

Something true.

"Again," she whispered against his ear, her hands gripping his shoulders. "I want all of you."

All of him. If she only knew what she was asking for.

But Colt gave her what she wanted, what they both needed, until the small space filled with the sound of skin against skin and breathless pleas and his name falling from her lips like a benediction. She took everything he had to give and demanded more, fearless in her want, and when she finally shattered beneath him for the second time, she took him with her.

He came hard, harder than he had ever in years, his body going rigid as everything he'd been holding back tore loose. Fuck. The release left him shaking, raw, like he'd been turned inside out. Two days of building tension, and now this—her skin, her heat, the way she'd said his name like it mattered.

He felt split open. Exposed. Like she'd reached inside his chest and rearranged something vital.

When it was over, he collapsed beside her on the narrow cot, both of them breathing hard in the firelight. Sloan's head was on his shoulder, her hair spilled across his chest, and Colt had never felt anything as perfect as the weight of her against him.

Which was exactly why he had to let her go.

The thought hit him like cold water, reality crashing back with brutal clarity. What had he done? What the hell had he been thinking?

He hadn't been thinking. That was the problem. He'd let three years of isolation and want override every rational thought in his head, and now Sloan was curled against him like she belonged there, like this meant something more than just two lonely people seeking comfort in a storm.

"This was a mistake." The words tasted like ash in his mouth.

Sloan went very still. "What?"

"This. Us. It was a mistake."

She lifted her head to look at him, and the expression on her face made his chest tight. "Why?"

"This is terrifying," he said finally.

"Why?"

"Because I want things I haven't wanted in years. Because you make me believe I might deserve them."

"You do deserve them."

"I'm falling for you," he said quietly. "I know it's too fast, I know it's—"

"I'm already gone," she interrupted. "Fell the moment you made me coffee like it was the most natural thing in the world."

His smile was soft, wondering. "What would it look like if I came back to work? Not hiding anymore?"

"What do you mean?"

"Trail crew. Building things that matter instead of just maintaining what's already broken."

Because you're a therapist and I'm your patient. Because you have a life worth living and I'm just marking time until I die. Because you touched my scars like they were beautiful and I know better than to believe in fairy tales.

"Because you're leaving," he said instead.

"Tomorrow. My 72 hours will be up."

"So this doesn't change anything. You'll hike down that mountain and file your report, and I'll still be up here."

"It doesn't have to be that way."

Colt sat up, running a hand through his hair. The movement made his side pull, the brand aching like it always did when he was stressed. "Yes, it does."

"Why?" Sloan sat up too, completely unselfconscious in her nakedness. "Why does it have to be that way?"

"Because that's how it is." He reached for his jeans, needing the armor of clothing between them. "You're a therapist. I'm not your fucking project."

The words hit their mark. He saw her flinch, saw hurt flash across her features before she pulled her own walls back into place.

"Is that what you think this was?" Her voice was carefully controlled now, professional. "Me trying to fix you?"

"Wasn't it?"

Sloan stared at him for a long moment, then reached for the flannel shirt. When she pulled it on, Colt felt the loss like a physical ache.

"You know what?" She stood up, moving to her pack with deliberate calm. "You're right. This was a mistake."

Colt told himself the relief he felt was genuine. This was better. Cleaner. She could leave without any messy complications, and he could go back to the life he'd built for himself up here.

So why did it feel like his chest was caving in?

"Sloan—"

"Don't." She held up a hand, not looking at him. "Just... don't."

The silence stretched between them, heavy with all the things they weren't saying. Outside, the storm was finally moving through, the rain gentling to a whisper against the windows.

"I'll finish my assessment in the morning and hike out," Sloan said finally.

Colt nodded, not trusting his voice.

She settled back onto her sleeping bag on the floor, as far from the cot as the small space would allow. The message was clear: whatever had just happened between them was over.

Colt lay back down and stared at the ceiling, listening to the sound of her breathing as it gradually evened out into sleep. His body still hummed with the memory of her touch, the phantom weight of her against him, and he knew with brutal certainty that he'd just made the biggest mistake of his life.

Not sleeping with her.

Letting her go.

# 5

## AFTER THE BURN

**SLOAN**

S loan lay on her sleeping bag and tried not to cry.

She'd had casual sex before. She'd had relationships that ended badly, men who'd used her and discarded her, heartbreaks that had taken months to get over. But nothing had prepared her for the whiplash of the last hour.

One moment, Colt had been kissing her like she was the answer to every prayer he'd never said, taking her apart with a desperation that matched her own. The next, he was pushing her away like she was just another problem to be solved.

*You're a therapist. I'm not your fucking project.*

The words echoed in her head, each repetition like a fresh cut. Was that really what he thought? That she'd slept with him out of some misguided attempt at therapy?

Maybe he wasn't entirely wrong. She'd crossed every professional boundary in the book tonight, let her personal feelings override her training, and her common sense. She'd touched a client—kissed a client, fucked a client—and told herself it was about connection, about healing, about two people finding solace in each other.

But lying here in the dark with her body still humming from his touch, Sloan had to admit the truth: she'd wanted him from the moment she'd seen him swinging that axe, shirtless and scowling in the afternoon sun. Everything else—the professional concern, the therapeutic instincts—had just been window dressing on simple, devastating attraction.

And somehow, Colt had seen right through her.

She rolled onto her side, facing away from the cot where he lay silent and still. She could feel his wakefulness like a weight on her back, but neither of them spoke. What was there to say?

Sorry for crossing professional boundaries?

Sorry for wanting you so badly I forgot my own name?

Sorry for thinking this might mean something to you?

Sloan closed her eyes and tried to focus on her breathing, on the practical details of tomorrow's hike, on anything other than the way Colt had looked at her when she'd touched his scars. Like she was seeing him—really seeing him—for the first time in years.

But that had been an illusion, clearly. Because if he'd really felt seen, really felt connected, he wouldn't have been so quick to dismiss what had happened between them as a mistake.

The worst part was that he was probably right. She was leaving. She did have a life in town, a job that required her to maintain professional distance. And he was staying up here, locked in his self-imposed exile with nothing but his guilt and his scars for company.

There was no future in this. No happy ending waiting at the bottom of the mountain.

But God, for a few minutes there, she'd almost believed there could be.

Sloan pulled the sleeping bag up to her chin and tried to pretend the dampness on her cheeks was just condensation from the cooling air. Tomorrow she'd hike down, file her report, and move on to the next assignment. Tonight had been an aberration, a moment of weakness she couldn't afford to repeat.

Professional distance. She really was going to have to work on that.

Behind her, she heard Colt shift on the narrow cot, and for a moment, she thought he might say something. Apologize, maybe, or try to explain why he'd pushed her away so cruelly.

Instead, she heard the soft whisper of fabric against skin, and she knew he'd turned away from her too.

The fire in the stove burned down to embers, and the tower grew cold around them. But the chill in the air was nothing compared to the ice that had settled in Sloan's chest, right where hope used to live.

SLOAN WOKE to the sound of Colt moving around the tower with deliberate quiet, like he was trying not to wake her. She kept her eyes closed and listened to him check the radio for weather updates, then move to the window to assess the clearing skies.

The morning light filtering through the windows was clear and bright—no more storms on the horizon. Perfect hiking weather. The kind of day that would let her complete her 72-hour assessment and file her report.

The kind of day that would let her leave, if that's what she wanted.

She sat up, and Colt's movements went completely still.

"Morning," she said, her voice carefully neutral.

"Morning." He didn't look at her, just continued checking his weather instruments with unnecessary focus. "Storm systems moved through. Should be clear for the next few days."

There it was—that edge in his voice, like he was already putting distance between them. After last night, after he'd shown her his brand and told her about Marcus, he was retreating back into himself.

"Good," she said, testing him. "I can finish my assessment today and hike out tomorrow."

Something flickered across his face—relief or disappointment, she couldn't tell. "Right. Your job."

"Yes, my job." She stood up, brushing her hair back from her face. "The thing that brought me here."

"The thing that's taking you away."

The words came out more bitter than he'd probably intended, and Sloan felt something twist in her chest. "It doesn't have to."

Colt finally looked at her, and the expression on his face was carefully blank. "Doesn't it?"

"I don't know. You tell me."

For a moment, she thought he might actually answer. Might crack open that careful control and tell her what he was really thinking. Instead, he turned back to the window.

"Weather's clear. You should pack."

The dismissal stung more than it should have. After everything they'd shared last night—his story about Marcus, the way he'd let her touch his scars, the raw honesty in his voice when he'd admitted he didn't know how to stop punishing himself—he was shutting her out again.

"You're doing it again," she said quietly.

"Doing what?"

"Pushing me away because you're scared."

Colt's jaw tightened. "I'm not scared."

"Then what are you?"

"Realistic." He moved away from the window, putting more distance between them. "You have a life down there. A job that matters. People who need you."

"And you don't think you need me?"

"I know I don't deserve you."

The words hit her like a physical blow. Sloan felt something crack in her chest, a pain so sharp it took her breath away.

"Who made you feel like this?" she asked softly.

Colt's face shuttered. "Nobody had to make me feel anything. I know what I am."

"And what's that?"

"Someone who gets the people he cares about killed."

"That's not true."

"It is." His voice was flat, certain. "You want to know the real story? The one I didn't tell you last night?"

"Yes."

Colt was quiet for a long moment, and she could see him weighing his options. Tell her the whole truth and watch her run, or keep lying and drive her away anyway.

"Someone who gets the people he cares about killed."

"That's not true." "It is." His voice was flat, certain.

"You know what happened. You know why I'm up here."

"I know you've been punishing yourself for three years for something that wasn't your fault."

"It was my fault."

"Making a desperate decision in an impossible situation doesn't make you a killer, Colt."

# HER TRAIL

COLT

C olt listened to the sound of Sloan packing her gear.

She moved with quiet efficiency, rolling up her sleeping bag and organizing her equipment with the same professional competence she'd shown when she'd first arrived. But there was something different in her movements now —a finality that made his chest tight.

Her 72 hours were up. Time to go.

He watched her, memorizing the way she moved in the early morning light. The careful way she folded her clothes. The methodical check of her pack. The professional mask that had slipped back into place sometime during the night.

"Weather's clear. Perfect hiking conditions." She shouldered her pack, testing the weight. "I should be able to make good time down the mountain."

Should be able to. Like she couldn't wait to get away from him.

Colt sat up slowly, his left leg protesting the movement. The old injury always acted up when storms rolled through, and three days of tension hadn't helped. "Your report?"

"I'll file it when I get back to town." She finally looked at him, and her expression was carefully neutral. "Standard assessment. You're physically healthy, mentally competent, able to perform your duties."

"That's it?"

"What else would there be?"

Everything, he wanted to say. The way you touched my scars like they were beautiful. The way you called me on my bullshit. The way you made me believe, for just a few hours, that I might be worth saving.

"Nothing," he said instead.

Sloan nodded and moved toward the door. "Take care of yourself, Colt."

The words were professional, polite, completely devoid of the warmth that had been in her voice two days ago when she'd traced his brand with gentle fingers. When she'd told him it didn't define him.

He should let her go. Should watch her walk away and be grateful that she wasn't going to put his failures in some government file. Should go back to his carefully constructed isolation and pretend the last three days had never happened.

Instead, he found himself getting up, pulling on boots and a jacket, following her down the stairs.

"What are you doing?" Sloan asked when she noticed him behind her.

"Making sure you get down safe."

"I don't need an escort."

"I know." But he kept following, maintaining distance but staying close enough to help if she needed it. Close enough to pretend he was still protecting something that mattered.

They hiked in silence for the first mile, the only sounds their boots on the trail and the rustle of wind through the trees. The path was clear, the storm damage minimal this high up. She'd have no trouble making it to her car.

Halfway down the ridge, Sloan stopped and turned to face him.

"Why are you here, Colt?"

Because I can't let you go. Because watching you walk away feels like dying. Because I'm a selfish bastard who wants what he can't have.

"Making sure you're safe," he said.

"I told you, I don't need—"

"I know what you told me." He stepped closer, close enough to see the gold flecks in her brown eyes. "But I'm here anyway."

"Why?"

The question hung in the air between them, loaded with everything they hadn't said. Everything they'd shared and thrown away in the space of a few hours.

"Because I'm going to miss you," he admitted.

Sloan's face went soft, and for a moment, she looked like the woman who'd touched his scars with reverent fingers. Who'd kissed him like he was worth saving.

"Then why did you push me away?"

"Because missing you is better than getting you killed."

The words came out harsh, desperate, and Sloan took a step back like he'd slapped her.

"You really believe that, don't you? That everyone you care about gets hurt."

"I know they do."

"Marcus again."

"Marcus always."

Sloan was quiet for a long moment, studying his face. When she spoke, her voice was gentle, understanding.

"You were partners," she said.

"That's what partners do. They save each other."

"He saved me. I got him killed."

"You both made the same decision. You both took the same risk. The only difference is luck."

"Luck." Colt laughed, the sound bitter and broken. "You call it luck that the better man died and the failure lived?"

"I call it tragedy. I call it the kind of random cruelty that happens in dangerous jobs." Her voice was steady, certain. "I don't call it your fault."

"You don't understand—"

"I understand perfectly."

She reached into her jacket pocket and pulled out a business card.

"My number. Not my work number. My personal one."

Colt stared at the card like it might bite him. "Why?"

"Because I'm not giving up on you."

"You should."

"Maybe. But I'm not." She pressed the card into his hand, her fingers warm against his palm. "If you ever want to stop punishing yourself. If you ever decide Marcus would want you to live instead of just exist. Call me."

"Sloan—"

"I mean it." Her voice was fierce, determined. "I'll be waiting."

She turned and started down the trail again, moving with renewed purpose. Colt watched her go, the business card burning in his hand like a brand of its own.

This time, he didn't follow.

But as her figure disappeared around a bend in the trail, he found himself thinking about what she'd said. About Marcus wanting him to live instead of just exist.

About the possibility that maybe, just maybe, she was right.

## SLOAN

Two weeks later, Sloan was sitting in her office in town, staring at a report she couldn't seem to finish writing.

*Subject displays signs of chronic isolation and unresolved trauma related to the death of a colleague. However, he appears physically healthy and competent in his current role. His living conditions are adequate, and he has made significant improvements to the fire tower infrastructure.*

*While subject would benefit from professional counseling, he is not an immediate danger to himself or others. Recommend follow-up assessment in six months.*

The words looked stark and clinical on the page, completely inadequate to capture the reality of Colt Ramsey. How did you write about the way he'd touched her like she was precious? How did you quantify the careful way he'd made her coffee, the protective stance he'd taken whenever she'd moved too close to the platform's edge?

How did you put heartbreak into a government form?

It was a lie, and they both knew it. Colt needed help—real help, not the kind of band-aid therapy she could provide during a routine check-in. But forcing him into treatment wouldn't save him. It would just drive him deeper into the mountains, further from any chance of healing.

She had to believe he'd come to that realization on his own. Had to believe the man who'd held her so carefully wasn't completely lost to his own guilt.

Her phone buzzed with a text message, and for a split second, her heart jumped. But it was just her supervisor, asking about the status of her report.

*Almost finished,* she typed back, then stared at the screen until the words blurred.

She'd checked her phone approximately five hundred times in the last two weeks. Had jumped every time it rang, hoping to hear a familiar rough voice on the other end. But Colt hadn't called. Hadn't even sent a smoke signal.

Maybe he'd thrown the card away the moment she'd turned her back. Maybe he'd decided she really was just another clueless professional trying to fix what couldn't be fixed.

Or maybe he was exactly where she'd left him—sitting in that fire tower, staring out at the mountains and convincing himself he didn't deserve anything good.

Her computer chimed with an email from the Forest Service. Another assignment, another isolated worker who needed checking on. She opened it automatically, scanning the details with professional detachment.

Then she saw the location, and her blood went cold.

*Bitterroot Ridge Fire Tower. Follow-up assessment requested for C. Ramsey. Complainant reports unusual activity—construction sounds, vehicle traffic. Possible unauthorized personnel on site.*

Sloan was out of her chair and reaching for her pack before she'd finished reading.

Construction sounds. Vehicle traffic.

Either Colt had finally snapped completely, or something was very wrong on that mountain.

She was two hours into the drive to the trailhead when she realized what she was really afraid of. Not that Colt was in trouble.

That he wasn't.

That he'd moved on, found someone else to share his carefully

rebuilt world. Someone who didn't come with professional obliga-
tions and ethical boundaries.

Someone better suited to the life he'd chosen.

But as Sloan pulled into the empty parking area and shouldered her pack for the hike up to the tower, she knew the truth.
She wasn't driving up here because of the report. She wasn't even
driving up here because she was worried about Colt's safety.

She was driving up here because two weeks without him felt
like two years, and she was tired of pretending she didn't care
what happened to the broken, beautiful man who'd branded
himself into her heart.

The trail seemed longer this time, each switchback a reminder
of the last time she'd made this climb. But when she finally crested
the ridge and saw the fire tower, Sloan stopped dead in her tracks.

Someone had been busy.

The structure looked the same from a distance, but as she got
closer, she could see the additions. A small cabin nestled against
the base of the tower, its walls fresh-cut timber that gleamed
golden in the afternoon sun. A covered porch with two chairs side
by side. A garden plot, carefully tended and protected by chicken
wire.

It looked like a home. Like a place where two people might
build a life together.

And carved into the support beam near the cabin door was a
symbol she recognized—the same mountain outline she'd traced
in the condensation on his window weeks ago.

Sloan's heart was hammering as she climbed the last few yards
to the clearing. The sound of construction was coming from
behind the cabin—rhythmic hammering that suggested someone
working with steady concentration.

She rounded the corner and found Colt building what looked
like a workshop, his back to her as he fitted boards together with

practiced precision. He was shirtless despite the cool air, his skin gleaming with sweat, and Sloan could see the brand clearly now in the afternoon light.

But there was something different about the way he carried himself. Less hunched, less guarded. Like the weight he'd been carrying had shifted somehow, become something he could bear instead of something that was slowly crushing him.

He must have sensed her presence because he turned around slowly, his eyes meeting hers across the small distance between them.

For a moment, neither of them moved. Then Colt set down his hammer and straightened, and Sloan saw something in his face she'd never seen before.

Hope.

"You came back," he said, his voice rough with surprise and something that sounded dangerously like relief.

"Got a report about unusual activity up here." Sloan gestured toward the cabin, the garden, the clear evidence of someone planning to stay. "Care to explain?"

Colt was quiet for a long moment, his eyes never leaving her face. "I've been thinking about what you said. About Marcus. About what he'd want."

"And?"

"And I think he'd want me to stop being such a stubborn asshole."

Despite everything, Sloan felt her mouth curve into a smile. "That's a start."

"I built you something," Colt said, gesturing toward the cabin. "Thought maybe... if you ever wanted to come back..."

He trailed off, uncertainty creeping into his expression. Like he was suddenly realizing how presumptuous it was to build someone a home without asking first.

Sloan walked closer, taking in the careful craftsmanship, the attention to detail. "It's beautiful."

"It's not finished. Needs insulation, proper plumbing, about a dozen other things." Colt was talking faster now, nervous energy spilling out of him. "But the bones are good. Solid. Built to last."

"Built for two people."

"Yeah." He met her eyes, and she saw the question there. The hope he was trying not to show. "Built for two people."

Nash appeared on the cabin threshold three days later like he'd materialized from the forest itself. Colt tensed, old instincts kicking in, until he saw the familiar weathered face.

"About time you came down from that tower," Nash said, taking in the cabin construction, the obvious signs of life being built for two.

"Nash." Colt's voice was carefully neutral.

"Heard you had company. Thought I should meet the woman who got Colt Ramsey to rejoin the living."

Sloan appeared from inside, flour in her hair, completely at ease. "You must be Nash. I've heard about you."

Nash's eyes crinkled. "All bad, I hope."

"Mostly." Sloan grinned. "Coffee?"

"Don't mind if I do."

When they were alone on the porch, Nash got serious. "Crew misses you. Trail work's not the same without someone who actually gives a damn about craftsmanship."

"I'm not ready—"

"Didn't say you were. But when you are..." Nash looked around the cabin. "Building things that last. That's what you do, Colt. Always has been."

"Even after what happened?"

"Especially after. Marcus would've kicked your ass for hiding up here this long."

Colt's jaw tightened, but Nash wasn't wrong.

"Think about it," Nash said, standing. "Trail work starts up again in spring. Could use someone to teach the new guys how to build things right instead of fast."

Sloan reached out and traced the carved mountain symbol with her fingertip, the same reverent touch she'd used on his brand that first night. Something about the parallel felt right—both marks carved by trauma, both transformed into something that could mean home.

"How long have you been working on this?"

"Since the day you left."

"Two weeks."

"Two weeks, three days, and about sixteen hours." Colt's mouth quirked into something that wasn't quite a smile. "But who's counting?"

"You were."

"Yeah. I was."

Sloan turned to face him fully, taking in the nervous tension in his shoulders, the way his hands flexed and unflexed at his sides. "Why didn't you call?"

"Because I wanted to have something to offer you. Something real." He gestured toward the cabin, the workshop, the careful beginnings of a life built for more than one person. "Not just apologies and promises. Something you could touch."

"Colt—"

"I know it's not much. I know you have a job, a life down in the town. But I thought maybe..." He stopped, took a breath. "I thought maybe we could figure out how to make it work. If you wanted to."

Sloan looked at him—really looked at him. The guilt was still there, would probably always be there in some form. But underneath it was something new. Something that looked suspiciously like the man he might have been before the fire, before Marcus, before three years of self-imposed exile.

"What about your brand?" she asked quietly. "Your punishment?"

Colt's hand moved instinctively to his side, covering the scar through his shirt. "Still there. Still mine. But maybe... maybe it doesn't have to be the only thing that defines me."

"And if I said yes? If I said I wanted to try?"

"Then I'd probably have a heart attack from relief."

Sloan laughed, surprising herself. "That's not very romantic."

"Give me time. I'm out of practice."

She studied his face, seeing past the casual words to the vulnerability underneath. He was terrified she'd say no. Terrified she'd point out all the very reasonable obstacles between them and walk away again.

Instead, she stepped closer and placed her hand flat against his chest, right over his heart.

"I have vacation time saved up," she said. "Maybe I could stay for a while. Help you finish the cabin."

Colt's eyes went dark, and his hand covered hers. "How long is a while?"

"I don't know." She paused, watching his face. "How long do you want me?"

He hesitated, his throat working like he was trying to find the right words. "I don't know what I'm doing here," he said finally. "I don't know how to be with someone, don't know how to make this work. But I know I don't want you to leave. Not today, not next week, not ever." His voice dropped to a whisper. "Forever. I want you forever."

The honesty in his voice made her chest tight. "That's a long time."

"Not long enough."

Sloan rose up on her toes and kissed him, soft and sure and full of promise. When they broke apart, Colt rested his forehead against hers.

"I love you," he said quietly. "I know it's too soon, I know it's complicated, but I love you."

"I love you too."

The words came out easier than she'd expected, true and simple and right. Colt's arms tightened around her, and for the first time in two weeks, Sloan felt like she could breathe again.

"So," she said against his mouth. "Show me this cabin you built."

"It's not much to look at yet."

"I don't care."

Colt pulled back to look at her, and the smile that spread across his face was like sunrise after a long, dark winter. "Come on, then. Let me show you your home."

7

---

# BRANDED

**SLOAN**

Four months later, Sloan woke in the cabin Colt had built for them to the sound of voices outside. Male voices, unfamiliar, and definitely not supposed to be there.

She rolled over, reaching for Colt, but found only empty space and cold sheets. Through the window, she could see him standing in the clearing with three other men, all of them wearing the same rugged uniform of flannel and work boots that marked them as trail crew.

One of them—a tall, broad-shouldered man with graying hair—was gesturing toward the cabin with obvious approval. Another, younger and dark-haired, was grinning at something Colt had said. The third looked like he'd rather be anywhere else, his arms crossed and his expression carefully neutral.

Sloan pulled on jeans and one of Colt's flannels, then stepped out onto the porch they'd finished just last week. The conversation stopped as all four men turned to look at her.

"Morning," she said, suddenly self-conscious about her bed hair and bare feet.

Three years alone, and now this. A woman who moved through his space like she belonged there.

"Sloan." Colt's voice was warm, proud, and when he looked at her, she saw something in his eyes that made her chest tight with happiness. "Come meet the crew."

The older man stepped forward first, extending a calloused hand.

"Nash. Trail boss. Heard a lot about you."

"All good, I hope."

"Mostly." Nash's weathered face cracked into a grin. "Colt says you're the reason he's not living like a hermit anymore."

The dark-haired man behind him stepped up with an easy smile that was pure trouble. "Sawyer. Nash's right hand and the crew's comic relief." His grin was infectious, the kind that made you want to know what mischief he was planning. "Also single, charming, and available for anyone who might know similarly qualified women."

"Subtle," Nash said dryly.

"I don't do subtle. Life's too short." Sawyer's eyes twinkled. "Plus, someone's got to balance out all the brooding mountain man energy around here."

"You thinking about coming back to the crew?" Nash asked Colt.

Colt glanced at Sloan. "Maybe. Part time. If someone can handle me being less than perfectly reliable."

"Hell," Sawyer said, "reliable's overrated. What matters is showing up when it counts." His grin widened. "Plus, we could use someone to teach the new guys how to build things right instead of fast."

"Sounds like you might have found your next project," Sloan said, squeezing Colt's hand.

As the crew prepared to leave, Nash turned back. "Trail work starts up again in spring. If you ever want to see what we're building down there..." He gestured toward the valley. "Door's always open."

"They came to check on the tower," Colt explained, his hand finding the small of her back. "Make sure I haven't completely lost my mind up here."

"Have you?" Nash asked, looking around at the cabin, the workshop, the neat garden plot that was already showing green shoots.

"Probably." Colt's arm tightened around Sloan's waist. "But in a good way."

Nash nodded approvingly. "Place looks good. Solid work."

"Thanks."

"You thinking about coming back to the crew?" Sawyer asked. "We could use someone with your experience."

Colt glanced at Sloan, and she could see him weighing the question. They'd talked about it—about what came next, how they'd build a life that worked for both of them. Her job was flexible; she could work remotely, make trips into town for the clients who needed face-to-face sessions. But Colt's future was still uncertain.

"Maybe," he said finally. "Part time. If Sloan's okay with it."

"It's your choice," she said, meaning it. "I'm not going anywhere."

The look he gave her was soft, grateful, full of the kind of love that still took her breath away. Four months, and she was still learning how to be loved by Colt Ramsey. Still discovering the man beneath the guilt and scars.

"Well," Nash said, clearing his throat. "We should let you two get back to your morning. Just wanted to see how you were settling in."

"And to extend an invitation," Sawyer added. "We're doing a holiday thing at the bunkhouse next month. Nothing fancy, just the crew and whoever wants to come. You two should join us."

"Christmas party?" Sloan asked.

"More like an excuse to drink too much and pretend we're civilized," Josh spoke up for the first time, his voice dry. "Fair warning—Sawyer gets sentimental when he's drunk."

"I do not."

"You cried during It's a Wonderful Life last year."

"That's a very moving film."

Despite his earlier reserve, Josh's mouth quirked into something that might have been a smile. "Anyway. You're welcome to come. Both of you."

"We'll think about it," Colt said.

After the crew left, Sloan and Colt sat on their porch with coffee, watching the morning mist burn off the valley below. It was peaceful, perfect, everything she'd never known she wanted.

"You should go," she said suddenly.

"Where?"

"The Christmas thing. With your crew."

Colt was quiet for a moment, turning his coffee mug in his hands. "I haven't been around people for Christmas in years."

"I know."

"What if I'm terrible at it? What if I don't remember how to be social?"

Sloan leaned against his shoulder, breathing in the scent of pine and sawdust that always clung to his clothes now. "Then you'll figure it out. And I'll be there to help."

"You want to go?"

"I want you to have the chance to reconnect with people who

matter to you." She tilted her head to look at him. "Besides, I'm curious about this crew you used to work with. Want to see you in your natural habitat."

"This is my natural habitat now." Colt gestured toward the cabin, the mountains, the life they'd built together. "With you."

"I know. But that doesn't mean you can't have both."

He was quiet for another long moment, then nodded slowly. "Okay. We'll go."

"Good." Sloan kissed his cheek, tasting coffee and the promise of winter. "It'll be fun."

"I doubt that." But Colt was smiling when he said it, and Sloan felt something settle in her chest. Another piece of the life they were building, another step toward the man he was becoming.


## COLT

Two weeks before the Christmas gathering, Colt was in his workshop, putting the finishing touches on a project he'd been working on for months. The wood was smooth under his hands, golden pine that he'd carved and sanded until it felt like silk.

But this wasn't just decorative carving. He'd used the brand—the same iron that had marked his failure—to burn a design into the wood. Sloan's mountain symbol, the one he'd seen her trace in the condensation on his window that first morning. The same symbol he'd carved into the cabin's support beam.

Turning his scar into something beautiful. His pain into a gift.

The irony wasn't lost on him.

"What's that?"

Colt looked up to find Sloan in the doorway of the workshop, her hair caught in the afternoon light. She was wearing one of his old work shirts over leggings, and the sight of her still made his chest tight with wonder. Four months, and he still couldn't quite believe she was real. Still couldn't believe she'd chosen to stay.

"Nothing," he said, covering the medallion with his hand.

"Liar." She stepped closer, trying to see around his arm. "Come on, show me."

"It's not finished."

"I don't care."

Colt hesitated, then moved his hand away. Sloan's eyes went wide when she saw the carved symbol, the careful detail of the mountains and trees. But when she reached for it, he pulled it back.

"Don't touch it yet. The finish is still wet."

"It's beautiful." Her voice was soft, wondering. "You made this?"

"Yeah."

"With your brand."

It wasn't a question, but Colt nodded anyway. "Seemed fitting. Taking something that was meant to mark failure and using it to create something else."

"What is it for?"

Colt felt heat creep up his neck. "You. It's for you."

"Colt—"

"I know it's not much. I know you could buy something better in town, something that didn't come with so much baggage attached. But I wanted to make you something that was mine. Something that came from here." He touched his chest, over his heart.

Sloan's eyes were bright, suspiciously bright, and when she spoke, her voice was rough. "It's perfect."

"You haven't even touched it yet."

"I don't need to. I can see how much love went into it."

Love. Such a simple word for something that had turned his entire world upside down. Colt still wasn't used to hearing it, wasn't used to believing he deserved it. But every day with Sloan made it a little easier.

"The back isn't done yet," he said, turning the medallion over to show her the smooth, uncarved surface. "Thought maybe you could tell me what to put there."

Sloan studied the blank wood, then looked up at him with an expression he couldn't quite read. "What do you want to put there?"

"I don't know. Your name, maybe. Or the date we met."

"What about his name?"

Colt went very still. "Whose name?"

"Marcus." Sloan's voice was gentle, careful. "He's part of this story too, isn't he? Part of what brought us together?"

The suggestion hit him like a physical blow. For four months, they'd barely talked about Marcus anymore, about the guilt that had driven Colt to the mountain in the first place. It was still there, would always be there, but it had transformed somehow. Become something he could carry instead of something that carried him.

"I don't know if I can," he said quietly.

"You don't have to. It was just a thought."

But the idea had taken root, and Colt found himself considering it. Marcus, whose death had led to the brand, which had led to the exile, which had led to Sloan. Marcus, who'd saved his life and inadvertently given him a chance at happiness he'd never thought he deserved.

"Maybe," he said finally. "Maybe that's exactly what should go there."

Sloan smiled, the kind of smile that lit up her whole face. "I think he'd like that. Being part of something beautiful instead of just something painful."

"Yeah." Colt touched the smooth wood, already imagining

Marcus's name carved into it with the same care he'd used for the mountains. "I think he would."

Later that night, as they lay in bed with the fire crackling in the wood stove, Sloan traced lazy patterns on Colt's chest. Her fingers found the brand through his shirt, as they often did, and she pressed her palm flat against it.

"Does it still hurt?" she asked.

"Sometimes. When the weather changes, or when I move wrong."

"I meant emotionally."

Colt considered the question. Four months ago, the answer would have been yes, always, like a wound that never healed. Now...

"Different kind of hurt," he said finally. "Less sharp. More like... remembering."

"Good remembering or bad remembering?"

"Both." He covered her hand with his, holding it against the scar. "But mostly good. Because it brought me here. To you."

"To us," Sloan corrected softly.

"To us."

Outside, the first snow of winter was starting to fall, dusting the mountains in white. But inside their cabin, warm and safe and together, Colt felt something he hadn't experienced in years.

Peace.

The medallion was finished a week later, Marcus's name carved into the back with the same care Colt had used for everything else. When he gave it to Sloan, she cried—the good kind of tears, the kind that meant healing instead of breaking.

She wore it to the Christmas gathering, the wooden pendant resting against her heart. And when Josh asked her about it—his voice carefully casual, like he was trying not to care—she told him the story. About the brand, about the mountain, about the man who'd learned to transform his scars into something beautiful.

Josh listened with the intensity of someone who understood more than he was saying. And when Sloan mentioned that she was a wilderness therapist, something shifted in his expression.

"Wilderness therapy," he repeated. "That's a real thing?"

"Very real. Why?"

Josh glanced around the room, taking in the crew scattered around the bunkhouse—Sawyer telling an elaborate story, Nash tending the fire, Colt watching it all with quiet contentment.

"No reason," he said finally. "Just curious."

But Sloan was a professional, and she recognized the signs. The careful questions, the guarded interest, the way Josh held himself apart even in a room full of people who clearly cared about him.

She tucked it away—not for her notes, not for a file, but for something quieter. The way she'd offered Colt a mirror instead of a rescue. The way she'd stayed.

After the holidays, maybe she'd hike up to Josh's cabin. Not to fix. Just to see if someone else needed to be seen.

After all, that's what she did. That's who she was.

And if there was one thing she'd learned from loving Colt Ramsey, it was that the most broken people often just needed someone willing to see past their scars to the whole person underneath.

Someone willing to stay long enough to watch them heal.


**EPILOGUE**

One year later, Sloan stood at the window of their cabin, watching Colt work in the garden they'd expanded together. He moved with easy confidence now, the haunted tension that had marked him when they'd first met replaced by something that looked suspiciously like contentment.

The brand was still there, would always be there. But it no longer defined him. It was just part of his story now—not the ending, but one chapter in a longer tale that included love and healing and the kind of happiness he'd never thought he deserved.

Her phone buzzed with a text from Nash. *Josh finally agreed to an assessment. Think you can work your magic again?*

Sloan smiled, her fingers moving to the wooden medallion at her throat. Marcus's name was worn smooth now from her touch, a reminder that sometimes the most broken things could become the most beautiful.

*On my way,* she typed back.

Outside, Colt looked up from his work and caught her watching. The smile he gave her was pure sunshine, free of shadows for the first time since she'd known him.

"Where are you going?" he called.

"To help someone else remember they're worth saving," she called back.

His grin widened. "That's my girl."

Yes, Sloan thought as she grabbed her pack and headed for the door. She was his girl. And he was her mountain man. And together, they were exactly what they were supposed to be.

Healed. Whole. Home.

The End

# THE VIRGIN MOUNTAIN MAN FALLS FIRST

## A CURVY GIRL REVERSE AGE GAP ROMANCE

# 1
———

MORGAN

The ranger barely looked up when she slid her ID across the counter.

"Cabin's shared-use," he said. "Someone's already up there."

Morgan didn't blink. "Anyone I need to worry about?"

He snorted. "Trail crew. Quiet type. Keeps to himself."

Perfect.

She took the key, the trail map, and a granola bar she didn't ask for.

"Anything else?"

"Just don't piss him off."

She headed out without asking for clarification. She didn't need it.

The cabin had a roof. Four walls. She wasn't here for luxury. She was here to breathe. To remember what it felt like to move her body for something other than survival.

She check the map. Six miles up. Minimal elevation. Basic terrain. She'd done harder.

The heat hit before she passed the second switchback—early fall sun thick enough to soak her T-shirt with sweat by the halfway mark. She stripped off her outer flannel and tied it around her waist, her chest rising harder than she liked.

Out of shape. Still soft. Still pissed that she cared.

The pack dug into her shoulders, her thighs burned with the incline, and her ponytail had sweat pooled at the base of her neck. The old Morgan—the one twenty pounds lighter and one broken marriage ago—would've kept her head down and pushed through in silence.

That Morgan had bent over backwards to be easy. To be desirable. And when it fell apart, all she got was silence, a younger model, and a note that said, "It's not you."

This Morgan didn't need to be adored. She just needed air.

She stopped. Took a long drink of warm water. Then flipped the mountain the finger and kept going.

LYNX

He heard her before he saw her.

Boots scraping stone. Breathing hard. Water bottle sloshing in her side pocket like she hadn't tightened the cap. Her pace was uneven—one leg dragging a little more than the other near the top.

He stopped hammering. Let the last stake hang crooked while he stepped away from the cabin and into the edge of the trees.

Then he saw her.

Curvy. Flushed. Flannel around her waist. T-shirt soaked

between her breasts, sticking to her stomach and clinging in ways that made his throat tighten.

She wasn't young. Not like him.

The ones who passed through never saw him—not really. Just the quiet kid with tools. The muscle. The grunt. No one had ever looked at him like he could undo them. Until now. Not like the others that passed through here in filtered groups and matching hiking gear. No—she was real. And she looked like she didn't want anyone's goddamn approval for it.

His pulse kicked. Hard.

She paused at the edge of the clearing, hands on her hips, head tipped back, eyes shut like she needed one clean breath before going inside. The wind threaded through the trees like a breath held too long. Somewhere nearby, a raven cawed—a deep, throaty echo that reminded her how far she was from anything she could control.

She didn't see him.

He didn't move.

The shirt she wore had ridden up, flashing the curve of her belly. Sweat had soaked into the ends of her ponytail, curling them against her neck. And that ass—

He turned away, jaw tight.

"You the crew guy?"

Her voice snapped through the clearing like she owned it. She was closer than he expected. And when he looked up, her eyes were on him.

Hazel. Sharp. Curious.

He nodded. "Lincoln Shaw."

She huffed. "Of course, it's a full name. You don't look like a Lincoln."

He shrugged, dragging his gloves off slowly. "Everyone calls me Lynx."

Her gaze dropped to his hands. Then lower.

He saw the moment she noticed the sweat on his collarbone, the tool belt, the way his shirt clung to his chest. Her eyes widened —just a flicker—and then she smiled.

Not sweet. Not flirty.

Dangerous.

"Well, Lynx," she said, stepping past him toward the porch, "I hope you don't mind company. Because I'm not hiking back down."

MORGAN

The cabin was smaller than she remembered.

Wooden bunk frame in one corner. Old table, two chairs. Dry sink. A shelf stacked with a tin of matches, a roll of paper towels, and what looked like duct tape and shame.

She dropped her pack near the table and peeled her shirt off her back, the cotton clinging like a second skin. She tugged it free, grimacing as the sweat cooled on her skin.

No mirror. Good. She didn't want to see what her sports bra was doing to her cleavage, anyway.

Behind her, Lynx made a sound. Low. Throat-cleared.

She glanced over her shoulder.

He was frozen. Still near the door, boots planted wide, jaw tight like he was trying to swallow something sharp.

"You're not shy, are you?" she asked, voice light.

He blinked. "No."

Then nothing.

No comment. No leer. Just that damn stare.

She turned back toward the table and grabbed the water jug, pouring herself a cup with shaking hands. Her skin felt too hot. Her thighs ached from the hike and she hated the way the waistband of her leggings cut into her.

And still... his eyes hadn't moved.

"You always look at women like that?" she asked.

Silence.

Then a quiet, "No."

She faced him.

"You always look like that?"

She wasn't sure if he meant the flush in her cheeks or the way she was still breathing hard—or maybe the way her stomach curved out a little more than she'd like when she exhaled.

"Like what?" she asked.

He didn't answer. Just dropped his eyes like they'd given him away.

LYNX

She laid out her bedroll on the floor like it was nothing.

Knees bent, back flat as she smoothed the old sleeping pad, her hips swaying with every reach. He turned away, stacked tools he didn't need. Anything to keep his hands busy—anything to stop him from staring at the way her ass moved when she crawled.

"You can take the bunk," he said without turning.

"No thanks," she replied. "You were here first."

"I'm not gonna let you sleep on the floor."

She glanced up. One brow arched. "Why not? Afraid I'll melt?"

"No," he said. "Afraid you'll hate me when your spine locks up tomorrow."

She smiled. Not soft. Not coy. Just amused. And that was somehow worse.

It made her beautiful.

She stood, dusting her palms off on her thighs. "We could share it."

His heart kicked. Hard.

She was teasing. He knew that. The grin said so. But his body didn't give a shit. His fists curled before he could stop them. He didn't move. Didn't even blink.

"You'd hate that more than the floor," he said, voice flat.

She tilted her head. "You're probably right."

The silence between them thickened, pulled tight at the edges.

She broke it. "You're young, Lynx. But you don't stare like a boy."

And then she turned away—like she hadn't just broken his self-control into splinters. Most people treated his quiet like emptiness. She treated it like restraint. Like it meant something.

## 2

———————

MORGAN
She woke to the rhythmic crack-thud of something heavy splitting open.

The amber sunlight pierced through the weathered cabin slats, casting honeyed patterns across the rough-hewn floor. Early fall morning brought with it a crisp, knife-edged chill and profound silence, interrupted only by the rhythmic thwack of an axe splitting wood just beyond the pine door. She rolled onto her side, stiff from the floor, and winced as her hips protested. Her thighs ached in the best way, but her spine felt like it tender.

She sat up slowly, pulling on the same shirt from yesterday. Still damp. Still wrinkled. Still smelled faintly like nerves.

Outside, the sound continued. Crack. Thud. Crack. Thud.

She opened the door and stepped out barefoot, bracing her hands on the rail.

The air was sharp with pine and wood smoke. The old boards under her feet creaked like they remembered every step ever taken across them.

And froze.

He was shirtless.

Axe in hand. Body bent. Muscles stretched and slick with effort. His pants rode low on his hips, and his back flexed with every movement. The kind of back that didn't belong to a twenty-three-year-old. It belonged to a man who worked. Who carried weight.

He hadn't seen her yet. Or maybe he had and didn't care.

She watched his arms rise, the axe angle down, and the log snap clean.

Men like him—young, strong, uncomplicated—they wanted. They didn't stay.

She'd been touched like a trophy before. Worshiped for a few months, then left with a handful of memories and a body that never forgot how it felt to be adored.

She had no interest in fulfilling someone's fantasy about dating an older woman. She just needed coffee.

Goddamn.

She should go back inside. Stop staring. Remember that she was fifteen years older and way out of bounds. Instead, she stayed there—feet bare, breath shallow—watching a man with cat eyes and quiet hands split her willpower wide open.

LYNX

He felt her eyes on him before she made a sound.

Didn't need to look to know she was watching—barefoot, arms crossed, shirt clinging to the curve of her stomach.

The last log cracked. He let the axe drop.

Turned slow.

She didn't move.

Her hair was a mess. Ponytail limp. One sleeve slipping off her shoulder. The pink flush across her chest looked fresh—not leftover from the hike.

"You want coffee?" he asked, voice rougher than he meant.

She blinked like he'd pulled her out of something.

"You make coffee?"

"I boil water. Put things in it. It's not poison."

That got a smile. The real kind. The kind that made something shift in his chest.

He walked past her up the steps, sweat cooling on his skin, her body heat like gravity as he brushed too close and refused to look down.

Inside, he set the kettle on the small propane burner and turned the dial.

She followed him in, slow. Close.

"Thanks," she breathed. "You didn't have to."

He didn't answer. Didn't trust what might come out of his mouth.

He was too hard. Too aware. Too fucking obsessed with the way her nipples pressed against the thin fabric of her shirt—no bra now, and God, he noticed.

"I saw you working," she said. "You're strong."

He stayed silent. Let it sit.

Then replied, "You're watching me now."

She didn't flinch.

"You're easy on the eyes."

And just like that—something cracked open. Small. Dangerous. Irreversible.

## MORGAN

The cabin smelled like burned pine and cheap instant coffee, but somehow it worked. Or maybe it was the man standing too close, jaw clenched, shirtless like it wasn't a goddamn problem.

She grabbed two cups, then poured the coffee.

No sugar. No milk. No small talk.

Just heat.

She handed him one and caught the edge of his fingers against hers—rough, calloused, slow to pull away.

"Thanks," he said.

His voice was lower in the morning. Like smoke. Or something that burned slower and deeper than it should.

She leaned against the table and sipped her cup, trying not to flinch at the bitterness. He didn't flinch. Just drank it straight like it didn't bother him.

A drop slid down her cup, over her knuckle.

She licked it away.

Slow.

Instinct.

Then caught the look on his face and felt it everywhere.

He didn't blink. Didn't move. Just stared—those cat eyes locked to her mouth. "You good?" she asked, letting her voice dip a little lower.

He swallowed hard. Nodded once.

"You always stare like that?"

His jaw flexed.

"Only when I want something I know I shouldn't."

She gripped her cup tighter, the heat now below her skin, between her thighs, under every breath.

"You think I'm a mistake?"

His eyes dropped—finally—to her bare legs. Her thighs. Then back up.

"I think you're a lesson I'd like to learn the hard way."

LYNX

She was pushing now. Testing him.

Not with her hands—with her smile. With the way she arched her back against the table, sipping from that cup like it was wine, and she wanted to see what it would do to him.

It was working.

But he didn't move.

He watched.

Studied.

Measured the way her hip curved into the edge of the wood, the way her breasts rose when she breathed deep—like she was waiting for him to snap.

He wasn't going to snap.

He was going to drag it out until she begged for it.

"You always this serious?" she asked, still holding his stare.

"You always this dangerous?" he answered.

Her lips parted—just a little. She wasn't expecting that.

She tipped her head. "Dangerous, how?"

He took a step closer. Not touching. Not even near enough for heat. Just enough for her to feel it.

"Because I want to do things to you that don't match the way you're smiling at me."

She froze.

No comeback.

No teasing.

Her thighs pressed tighter. Her hand clenched the cup harder. And he saw the way her nipples peaked under the shirt.

"I'm too old for you," she said, but her voice had lost all its teeth.

He shook his head.

"You're exactly what I want."

She licked her bottom lip. Then tried again.

"I'm not looking for—"

He stepped in close.

Still not touching. Not yet.

"Then stop looking. I'm right here."

# 3

MORGAN

He'd gone back outside—silent and shirtless, stacking the last of the firewood like he hadn't just said the most dangerous thing she'd heard in five years.

Morgan stood inside, back to the bunk, trying to get her breathing under control. Her shirt stuck to her like it had melted there. Her thighs were still tacky from the sweat of the hike and the way he looked at her like he could smell her want on the air.

She pulled her top over her head and let it drop.

Paused. Not a move. Not a sound.

Then reached for the clean tank from her pack. Soft cotton, low armholes. No bra.

She didn't hear the steps on the porch. Didn't hear the creak of the door.

But she felt him.

Eyes on her.

She turned halfway—shirt in her hand, breasts bare, sweat glistening between them.

And he was there.

Leaning in the doorway. Watching. Not even pretending to look away.

Her stomach flipped. Her thighs clenched. And she didn't cover herself.

"You just stand there watching women change?" she asked.

His voice was calm. Controlled.

"Only when they look like that."

She tugged the tank over her head, slow. No rush. No panic.

He didn't move.

Didn't apologize. Didn't leave.

She walked to the table, poured a cup of water, suddenly even more thirsty, and took a sip like she hadn't just been seen—fully, nakedly seen—for the first time in years.

"You're playing with fire, Lynx."

He stepped inside. Quiet. Lethal.

"Then why do you keep striking matches?"

LYNX

She didn't look away this time.

Not when he stepped inside all the way. Not when the door swung shut behind him and the hush took over again—the kind of hush that has nothing to do with quiet, and everything to do with tension.

She leaned against the table, arms crossed under her breasts like she needed the shield. Like she knew damn well what he was thinking.

He was done pretending.

Her hair was falling loose around her face. Her shirt hugged every curve. She wasn't trying to be sexy.

She just was.

"You ever actually touched a woman?" she asked. Casual. Cool. But her fingers gripped her arms a little tighter.

He exhaled slowly.

"No."

She blinked. Her mouth opened—closed again. Like she didn't expect him to admit it.

But he wasn't ashamed.

"Doesn't mean I haven't thought about it."

He took another step in.

"Doesn't mean I haven't imagined it. Every night."

Another step.

"On my back. Fist wrapped tight. Thinking about you."

Her breath caught. Sharp and soft.

"I didn't even know your name until yesterday."

"Didn't need your name to want you."

He was in front of her now. Not touching. Not begging.

Just close enough for her to see the hunger in his eyes—and know it wasn't new.

"I've wanted this for a long time," he said, voice low. "But I wasn't gonna take anything you didn't offer."

A beat passed.

Her eyes dropped to his mouth.

Then to his chest.

Then back to his mouth.

"What if I want to offer it now?" she asked, just above a whisper.

He didn't move.

"Then say it."

She stared up at him, breath trembling, lips parted.

"I want it."

He stepped forward. No space left now.

"Then I'm done pretending I don't."

MORGAN

She should've stopped it. She should've laughed. Should've blamed the altitude or hormones or the fact that she hadn't been touched in such a long time. But then he said he imagined it every night.

And now her mouth was dry. Her nipples tight under the thin tank, thighs aching for friction she hadn't chased in years.

He stood there, still as a stone and twice as heavy. His voice calm. His hands loose at his sides like he wasn't a virgin staring down a half-naked woman fifteen years his senior.

She looked up at him.

"What do you want?"

His throat worked. His eyes didn't blink.

"I want to see you. All of You.

"I want to take my time. Because I've waited too long.

"I want to taste you. Make you say my name. Feel you shake under me."

She swallowed.

He kept going.

"I want to touch you until you stop thinking about everyone who came before me.

"I want to make you come on my mouth, and then again while I'm inside you.

"And I want you to hear you say you're mine when I do."

Her knees nearly buckled.

"Lynx," she whispered, but it wasn't a warning. It was a prayer.

He stepped closer, lips a breath from her ear.

"Tell me to stop, and I will. But if you don't...I'm going to lay you down on that bunk, kiss every inch of your skin, and make you forget why you ever thought I was too young for this."

LYNX

She didn't say stop.

She reached for the hem of her shirt with fingers that trembled once—just once—and then pulled it off, slow. Deliberate. Like she'd made the decision and wasn't going to second-guess it.

He didn't breathe.

Her breasts were bare. Full. Heavy. The curve of her waist dipping into soft hips that made his hands curl without meaning to.

She stood there like a challenge.

"Show me," she said.

He moved before his brain caught up. Put one hand on her waist like he was afraid to push too hard. She didn't flinch. Just looked up at him, eyes wide, mouth parted.

"You're shaking," he said, voice low.

"So are you."

He smiled, soft and small.

"Not from fear."

He brushed her hair from her neck. Pressed his mouth to her shoulder, then even lower. One kiss at a time until she sighed—a real sigh, like she hadn't let herself breathe that deep in years.

"You're not too much," he whispered. "You're everything."

He guided her to the bunk with gentle hands. The mattress creaked under them, wood groaning like it knew how long it had been since a body moved like this in the dark. Sweat and sawdust clung to the air. She laid back, arms loose at her sides, eyes locked on his like she was giving him permission with every breath.

He undressed them both slowly. Not shy—but focused. He saw her watching his chest, his arms, the muscles she hadn't expected in someone so quiet.

He kissed her ankles. Her knees. The soft inside of her thigh.

"Lynx—"

"I want to remember how you taste before I ever touch you anywhere else."

And then he did.

Tongue soft, reverent, then deep. One hand on her thigh, the other on her belly, holding her still while she broke apart. She gasped. Clawed for the bunk rail. Moaned his name in a voice she didn't know she had. He moved with practiced precision like he knew exactly what he was doing, his dark eyes watching her every reaction.

She came fast—tight, hot, utterly wrecked. He stayed there, gentle through the aftershocks, lips brushing her inner thigh while she tried to remember how to speak.

Then he moved up, kissed her chest, her neck, her mouth.

"Want to stop me?" he asked.

She wrapped her legs around his hips.

"Don't you fucking dare."

# 4

MORGAN

She was still gasping when he kissed her again.

Not rushed. Not needy. Just... full.

His mouth was soft. His hands weren't. One on her waist, the other on her jaw like he was afraid she'd drift away if he didn't hold her still.

"Lynx," she whispered, dazed. "I need..."

She couldn't finish it.

He didn't need her to.

He kissed her again and rolled his hips between her thighs. She felt him—thick, hard, trembling. Pressed to her entrance but not pushing. Not yet.

"I don't want to hurt you," he murmured.

"You won't."

"I've never—"

She cupped his face. Made him look at her.

"Then let me show you how."

He nodded. Breath shallow. Sweat beading at his temple like he was holding back everything.

She guided him in.

Slow. Careful. Thick.

Her body stretched to fit him and her back arched, a moan breaking from her throat that didn't sound like her voice at all.

He stopped. Froze.

"You okay?"

"Don't stop. Just... don't stop."

He pushed in deeper, hips rocking, eyes locked on hers like he needed to see every flicker of feeling. He was shaking—shoulders, arms, his mouth hovering over hers like it was too much.

But he didn't let go.

He filled her slow, inch by inch until she was gasping and clutching his back, until his name left her lips like a plea and a promise in one.

"You're so tight," he groaned. "So warm. Fuck, Morgan—you fit me so well."

She wrapped her legs around him tighter and held him there, deep inside, claimed without words.

They moved together—slow. Sweaty. Deep enough to steal the breath from her lungs. No one had ever let him take up space like this. Not in words. Not in want. She let him fill her—and it felt like being claimed back.

And when he came, it wasn't with a shout or a roar.

It was with a whispered "Thank you" against her throat like she'd given him something he'd been starving for.

LYNX

She was still panting. Her chest rose against his, thighs slick and trembling around his hips.

But he didn't move.

He didn't pull out. Her arms stayed locked around him, her body still wrapped around his, the heat between them unbroken, and when he shifted—thick and unmoving—her breath caught like it was starting all over again.

"Jesus," she whispered. "You're still—?"

"Yeah."

He nuzzled her neck, kissed the hollow behind her ear. Her skin was damp. Sweet. Still shivering.

"I'm not done," he murmured.

She huffed a laugh. "You just came."

"Once."

He pulled back to look at her—her face flushed, eyes heavy, lips parted and red from his mouth. And she looked at him like she'd forgotten how good it could be.

"I want more," he said. "If you'll let me."

She stared up at him. Her palm traced down his back, then over his side, fingers curling around his hip.

"I should say no," she whispered. "I should let this be enough."

"But?"

Her thighs clenched around him again, hips lifting without thought.

"But you're still inside me, Lincoln."

His eyes burned at the sound of his name on her lips—not Lynx. Not a nickname. Him.

He kissed her slow. Deep. Then moved again.

She gasped, fingers digging into his shoulders.

"Harder," she whispered.

He gave her what she asked for.

"Faster."

He thrust deep, and her head tipped back, a moan ripping loose.

"More."

He grinned against her mouth, breath rough, cock still rock solid, hips pounding now.

"Yeah, sweetheart," he growled. "I've got more."

MORGAN

He was still inside her. Even after round two.

Still hard.

Still looking at her like she was the first sunrise he ever saw and the last one he ever needed.

She should've been sore enough to say no. Spent enough to roll over so she was on top, kiss him once, and pretend it hadn't meant more than it should.

Instead?

She rolled her hips. Slow. Deliberate.

She grinned—wicked, smug, still sore, but not sorry. "Thought you were the one with stamina," she teased.

He groaned, head falling back. "You're going to kill me."

"Not yet." She shifted again, slow and dirty. "I like you too much for that."

His breath left him in a rough sound that went straight to her core.

"Morgan..."

"You're young," she said. "But you're not delicate."

He opened his mouth like he might argue—so she moved again.

This time with purpose.

Her hands braced on his chest, her knees wide, her body sinking down around him with a heat that made them both shudder.

His hands flew to her hips. Tried to slow her. Hold her.

"You don't have to—"

"I want to," she said, cutting him off. "Let me."

His jaw went tight. His hands stayed on her. But he let go of control.

And she rode him.

Slow at first. Then faster. Then grinding, panting, moaning his name with every sharp thrust of her hips.

She watched him watch her—eyes wide, jaw slack, sweat beading at his temple like he couldn't believe what she was doing to him.

She was above him. Heavy, hot, home. Her thighs flexed around his ribs, and he knew—this wasn't a dream. It was memory being made, one thrust at a time.

"I'll dream about this. For the rest of my life."

She bent forward. Braced her hands on either side of his head. Her breasts brushed his chest with every movement.

"You gonna come again, mountain man?"

He nodded, breath wrecked.

She clenched around him—playful now, daring him to keep up. His hands flew to her hips like a man trying to survive a storm made of honey and heat.

"Then do it. Let me feel it."

And he did.

With a guttural moan and a kiss to her throat, he came so hard she felt it in every part of her.

LYNX

She collapsed on top of him, chest slick against his, her breath hot and uneven against his neck.

He didn't move.

Couldn't.

Not with the way her body still pulsed around him, not with the weight of her skin on his like a blanket he never wanted to shed.

One hand drifted to her back, tracing slow, aimless paths along her spine. Her shoulders. Down to the curve of her ass where he'd held her like he was afraid she might vanish mid-thrust.

"That was..." she whispered. But she didn't finish the sentence.

She didn't need to.

He kissed her hair. Just once. Let his fingers settle on her hips.

He stayed joined to her. Not thrusting. Not greedy. Just full. Still. Home.

Her head rested on his chest, ear to his heartbeat. Her hand splayed over his ribs. She didn't look at him. Didn't move to get up.

He didn't push for anything.

Except one thing.

"Stay the night," he murmured.

She was silent.

But she didn't get up.

Didn't shift away from his touch as his hands slid lower, to the dip of her waist. Over her thighs. Light touches, slow and focused —like he was memorizing her piece by piece.

And he was.

He traced the softness of her stomach, the lines of her hips, the small stretch marks that peeked from under the hem of the blanket. And he kissed them.

She didn't stop him. Couldn't. No one had touched her like this—not with reverence, not like the shape of her meant something. And if she let herself, she could almost believe it wasn't temporary.

One by one.

"You're perfect," he whispered.

She huffed something that was maybe a laugh. Maybe not.

"You're just drunk on sex."

"No. I'm drunk on you."

And when she finally looked up at him—really looked—he didn't smile.

He just stared back.

Open. Raw. Ruined.

Because now that he'd had her, he didn't know how he was supposed to go back to not having her again.

# 5

MORGAN

She woke up aching.

Not the kind of ache that came from hiking too hard or sleeping on uneven ground—no, this was deeper. Thicker. The kind of soreness that bloomed behind her knees and low in her belly. The kind that came from being filled, gripped, pulled apart, and put back together again.

She shifted under the quilt and winced.

Thighs tender. Core sore. Breasts heavy.

And underneath the ache?

Satisfaction. Raw. Dangerous.

A calloused hand slid over her waist. His breath warmed the back of her neck.

"You okay?" he murmured.

"I'm sore," she whispered.

"Good sore or bad?"

She didn't answer. Not right away.

Because it wasn't either.

It was too much. Too good. Too perfect. The kind of good that made her forget things like reason or age or how fast men like him changed their minds.

His hand didn't stop moving. He didn't grope. Didn't press. Just... touched. Slow. Careful.

His palm cupped her hip, thumb sweeping gently over the round edge of her ass. She felt the weight of his cock against her thigh—thick. Full. Hard.

"You're not done?" she asked, not even sure if it was teasing or terrified.

"Not even close," he said, voice gravel and heat. "But I'll wait. If you want."

He smoothed his hand over her stomach. Slow. Steady. "I didn't wait because I was scared," he said. ""I waited because nothing in my past ever felt important enough to risk ruining with something incomplete or half-hearted."

She went still.

"What we just did?" he murmured, lips brushing her neck. "That wasn't incomplete. That was everything."

She turned to face him fully. Brushed his hair off his forehead.

"So I wasn't your first option."

He shook his head.

"You were the first real one."

His eyes were on her.

Watching her.

Soft and sure.

"No one's ever touched me like that," she said before she could stop herself.

He didn't smile. Didn't gloat. Just stared at her like she was the only thing in the world that made sense.

"That's not gonna change," he said.

And the worst part? She wanted to believe him.

By the time she rolled out of bed again after falling asleep, her stomach was grumbling and her thighs were trembling. She tugged on his shirt—still rumpled from the night before—and padded barefoot to the tiny kitchenette.

"You're gonna burn that," she said, watching Lynx try to coax a flame out of the camp stove like it owed him money.

"I've made worse," he muttered.

She smirked and elbowed him aside. "Sit. Let me do it before you light the cabin on fire."

He didn't argue. Just sat at the table, watching her like she was something worth getting used to.

He set her mug down with quiet precision. Two hands. Like it mattered. Like she mattered. That part scared her more than the sex.

She made eggs. Burned the first batch of toast and laughed when he scraped it clean with a knife. "Gourmet," he said. "You're clearly trying to impress me."

She brought the plate over, dropped into his lap without warning, and kissed the line of his jaw.

"Not trying," she whispered. "Just staying."

Later, when he came back inside from working outside, she filled the basin with warm water and motioned for him to sit. "You've got dried sweat and bark in your hair, mountain man."

He raised an eyebrow but let her guide him down. She knelt behind him with a rag, washing the back of his neck, the slope of his shoulders, and the ridge of muscle along his spine.

"Jesus," he muttered, head dipping forward.

"You're not so tough," she said.

His voice dropped to a whisper. "Only when you're not touching me."

LYNX

She was watching him now. Like she couldn't decide if she wanted to run or climb on top of him.

So he waited.

Let her stare. Let her think. She moved in front of him.

His hand strayed to her hip, warm and steady. Her hair was tangled. Her lips still kissed raw. And the curve of her stomach rose and fell with every shaky breath she didn't seem to want him to notice.

"You can say no," he said again. "You don't have to prove anything."

She didn't answer. Just shifted, slow and deliberate, onto his lap. Her thighs parted. Her hand trailed down to rest between them.

"I don't want slow this time," she whispered. "I just want you."

His cock twitched at the sound of her voice—that rasp, that need, the quiet surrender tucked into every syllable. He got up and moved them to the bunk, her legs wrapping around where he needed her the most.

He rolled on top of her, chest to chest, keeping his weight on his arms, his hips hovering above hers. He undressed them both quickly, not wanting anything in his way.

"You're sure?"

"Yes," she breathed.

He pushed inside her slowly, but not timid. The stretch made her gasp, fingers flying to his arms, her nails biting into his biceps.

"God—Lynx—"

"I know, baby. I know."

He buried himself to the hilt, then held still. Let her adjust. Let her feel.

Then he moved.

Deep. Steady. Unrelenting.

His mouth found hers—tongue slow, kiss thoroughly. One of his hands cupped her face while the other locked her thigh around his hip.

"You're so tight," he groaned. "Like you were made to fuck me."

She whimpered. Her body clenched.

"You feel that? Every inch of you wrapped around me? That's you choosing me."

She moaned like the word mine undid her.

He fucked her slow, then faster, kissing every place he could reach—her neck, her breasts, her mouth, her jaw—like he had to memorize her again, just in case she changed her mind later.

"You gonna come for me?" he whispered. "Need you to."

She shattered on the next stroke.

Tight. Wet. Crying out his name like it hurt.

And when she clenched around him again, dragging him to the edge, he lost it—came hard and deep, his name still on her lips, her nails in his back.

He stayed inside her. Held her.

"Told you I wasn't done," he whispered, kissing her temple.

"I don't want you to be."

MORGAN

The third time should've felt excessive.

But it didn't.

It felt inevitable.

Her thighs trembled. Sweat slicked her chest—heat wasn't the reason. She lay limp, satisfied, thoroughly—obscenely—used in the best possible way.

But as Lynx drifted off, one hand still splayed over her stomach, Morgan stared at the ceiling. Every sensation and emotion she felt seemed like a truth she wasn't yet ready to acknowledge.

This wouldn't last. It couldn't.

She slid out of bed carefully, trying not to wake him. She should've kissed him. Should've stayed. But wanting this—him— meant risking more than her body. And she wasn't sure she knew how to want like that anymore. Her body protested with every movement—sore, stretched, marked. She felt him on her everywhere. Inside and out. Under her fingernails and in her fucking bloodstream.

She tugged his flannel over her head, rolled her shoulders, and tried to remember how to breathe without him watching her do it. If she stayed, she'd start believing in things she wasn't sure she could keep. Like warmth. Like worth. Like someone might actually want her without her needing to earn it first.

Coffee. Coffee would fix it.

She struck a match. Boiled the water. Opened the tin.

His mug was next to hers.

Of course it was.

She poured two cups anyway.

He came up behind her like a ghost—bare feet silent, hand brushing her hip.

"You always leave bed without saying goodbye?" he murmured, sleep-rough.

She smiled, but it didn't reach anything that mattered.

"Didn't want to wake you."

The silence between them wasn't heavy—it was full. Full of

things she wasn't ready to ask for. And maybe that was worse. Wanting more than he meant to give.

She handed him a mug and leaned against the counter, watching the steam rise.

"What happens now?"

He frowned. "Now?"

"When we get off this mountain."

"You tell me."

She shook her head. "You're twenty-three. You think this meant forever. But I know better."

"And what if I do think that?" he asked, voice low.

"Then you'll be disappointed."

He took a sip of coffee. Watched her over the rim.

"You're scared."

She looked away. "I'm practical."

"No," he said. "You're scared of what it means to be wanted like this."

She didn't answer.

Because he was right.

And that scared her more than anything.

LYNX

She moved like she'd already made her decision.

Didn't say much. Didn't meet his eyes. Just packed her things with mechanical precision—fold, stuff, zip. No hesitation. No softness.

She wore his flannel still. But she buttoned it all the way up. Covered the curve of her chest, the bruises on her thighs where his fingers had dug too hard. Where he'd held her like he couldn't let go. The flannel still smelled like him. Like pine and wood smoke and something dangerous, she didn't know how to keep. She could survive missing him. She wasn't sure she could survive hoping.

He watched her from the porch.

Said nothing.

Didn't ask her to stay. Didn't offer some speech he wasn't ready to give.

He just sat on the steps with a knife in one hand, a piece of trail pine in the other, and carved like it was the only way to keep from splitting open.

When she finally stepped out, pack strapped to her shoulders, she paused in front of him. For a second. Maybe less.

"Thanks for the bunk," she said, trying to keep it light—trying not to ask if he wanted her to stay.

He didn't smile.

"Thanks for... everything."

He nodded once.

Didn't trust his mouth to work right.

Then she walked down the trail.

Didn't look back.

But she found it an hour later.

Tucked into the side pocket of her pack.

A smooth piece of wood, palm-sized, worn from handling. On one side: a single carved phrase.

*Fall into me.*

Her hand tightened around it. Her feet stopped moving.

And somewhere in the woods below, Lynx was still waiting.

# 6

MORGAN

Her bed felt like a hotel room after a bad breakup—blank, overpriced, and one thread count too proud of itself. She missed the scrape of bark against her spine. Jesus. She missed him.

She lay flat on her back, one arm over her eyes, the other resting on her stomach—right where his hand used to be. The place he always landed in sleep. The way he'd pull her closer like she was something he'd claimed, not borrowed.

She hadn't slept since she left the cabin.

Not really.

Her body still ached. Not from the hike, but from the way he'd touched her like he wanted every inch to remember him.

And it did.

She still felt the stretch. The soreness. The echo of his cock inside her, thick and perfect and impossible to forget.

She rolled to her side and shoved her hand under her pillow.

The carving was there. She couldn't help it.

Smooth pine. Just wide enough to fit her palm.

*Fall into me.*

She stared at the words like they were a dare. Or maybe a promise. Or maybe the thing she should've done the moment she saw his eyes in the firelight and realized what they meant:

He hadn't fallen. He'd been waiting. And she'd walked away.

Now the apartment felt like a box. Her life, like something that didn't quite fit anymore. Her reflection looked older, duller. And no amount of coffee or cream or cover-up could hide the fact that her body wanted more.

More of him.

His voice. His hands. His praise. His ruin.

She dragged a blanket over her legs and closed her eyes. But all she saw was that look—when she was on top of him, when he came inside her, when he touched her like she was something he couldn't live without.

She clutched the carving harder. She kept thinking about the way his hands moved—slow, deliberate like everything he touched was meant to last. Even her.

Her fingers traced the grooves again, remembering the way his hands moved over her in the dark. The rasp of his voice in her ear. The way he said her name like a vow. How he looked at her when she rode him—like she was both salvation and sin.

She closed her eyes. But the firelight was still there behind her lids. His eyes glowing gold. And the carving, pressed into her palm, felt like a promise she'd already broken.

"Fuck," she whispered. "I made a mistake."

The next morning, Morgan tried to write him a note. Something smart. Something clear. Something that didn't sound like a confession.

She opened her journal and started three times:

"You were exactly what I needed."

"This isn't about you. It's about me."

"Don't wait for me."

Each one ended up scratched out. The pen tore through the page.

She closed the book, stared at the ceiling, and realized something awful:

She didn't want him to let her go. She called her sister.

"You sound like shit," her sister said through the phone.

"Thanks."

"Still thinking about that guy?" Silence. "You know you can want something good, right? You don't always have to be first out the door to keep control."

Morgan hung up before she could cry. And packed her bag before she could stop herself.

LYNX

He'd already seen her before she spoke. The woods had welcomed her back in silence. No birdsong this time—just wind in the trees and the rhythmic pulse of his heartbeat in his ears. It wasn't the trail that changed. It was her.

She stood just off the trail, backpack in one hand, the other fisted tight at her side like maybe if she let go, she'd run again.

He didn't move. Didn't wave. Just drove the pickaxe into the rocky patch of ground one more time. Hard. Sharp. Deep.

Then he straightened.

Waited.

She stepped into the clearing like it cost her something.

It probably did.

She didn't speak right away. Didn't smile. Just stood there like a woman who hadn't slept. Who hadn't been touched in two days and was losing her mind over it.

Good.

He was already gone.

"I couldn't stop thinking about you," she said finally.

He stared. She moved closer.

"Couldn't eat. Couldn't sleep."

Still nothing.

"I thought I could leave it there. You. The cabin. All of it."

She swallowed. Her eyes burned.

"I was wrong."

He wiped his hands slowly. Stepped toward her.

One foot. Then another.

Until they were toe to toe, heat rolling off both of them, the tension so thick it tasted like metal.

"Say it," he said. Low. Controlled. Dangerous.

He'd dreamed of this. Of her. A hundred ways she might come back. None of them looked like this—red-eyed and shaking. Real.

"Say you came back for me."

She looked up at him, voice shaking.

"I came back for you."

His hand snapped out. Gripped her waist. Pulled her in hard enough her breath caught.

"You gonna run again?"

"Not unless you make me."

He leaned down, his lips brushing her ear.

"I'll make you scream first."

And then he kissed her like he'd been starving since the second she left—tongue deep, teeth sharp, hands everywhere.

This time, he wasn't waiting.

MORGAN

She didn't remember moving.

One second she was standing in front of him, trying to speak around the knot in her throat—and the next, he had her pressed to a tree, mouth on her neck, hands under her shirt, ripping reality away one touch at a time.

Her back scraped rough bark. She didn't care. Her thighs were already wet, pulsing, spread around his hips like they'd never been anywhere else.

"You left," he growled.

His hand slipped between her legs, cupped her through her leggings. She gasped.

"You left," he said again, this time softer—wrecked.

"I'm sorry," she breathed. "I was scared."

"I know."

He kissed her. Brutal. Filthy. Perfect.

Then he dropped to his knees.

She barely got his name out—

"Lynx—"

—but his hands were already tugging her leggings down, baring her thighs, her cunt, her fucking soul.

He mouthed her through her panties. Licked her like it was a language. Tongue flat, slow. Then sharp and deep, like he needed to prove something.

"You taste like mine," he murmured.

She cried out, grabbed a fistful of his hair.

"You gonna run now?" he asked.

She shook her head. Didn't trust her voice.

He peeled her panties to the side, fingers sliding in with a groan.

"So fucking wet for me."

He stood in one smooth motion, shoved his jeans down just enough, and hooked her legs up around his hips.

"Hold on."

And then he slammed inside her.

She gasped—loud. The stretch, the angle, the fucking depth.

"God, Lynx—"

"You came back," he growled. He thrust deep, chest to hers, voice breaking on the next word. "You're mine now—if you still want to be."

She didn't hesitate. Wrapped her legs tighter, heart in her throat. "I never stopped."

He fucked her deep. Fast. Filthy. The bark scraped her spine. His hips slapped against hers. His hand clamped over her mouth when she moaned too loud.

"You feel that?" he panted. "That's me. Still hard for you. Still hungry."

She came first.

Legs shaking. Mouth full of his name. Her cunt clenching so tight he nearly dropped her.

Then he followed—deep and rough, teeth in her shoulder, hips grinding as he emptied himself inside her.

LYNX

She didn't speak. She clung to him—wrecked, breathless—her thighs locked tight around his waist, his cock still buried deep, pulsing in time with her heartbeat.

Good.

Because he wasn't letting her go again.

His chest was heaving. His cock still twitching inside her. Her cunt still fluttering around him in tiny aftershocks that made his knees threaten to give out all over again.

He turned slowly, backed up to a downed log, and sank onto it with her still wrapped around him. Still joined. Still claimed.

Her breath was warm against his throat.

"You okay?" he asked.

She didn't answer at first. Just nodded against his skin.

"That was..." she tried, then gave up.

"Yeah," he said, voice rough. "It was."

She shifted slightly, hissing, thighs sore and trembling. He tightened his grip.

"Don't move yet. Let me keep you like this."

"Still inside me," she whispered.

"Where I belong."

Her breath hitched.

He pulled back just enough to make her look at him.

"Don't leave again," he said, voice lower now.

She searched his face. Like she needed to be sure this wasn't just heat or adrenaline or obsession. Like she didn't already feel him in every damn part of her body.

"You sure about that?"

"You ran once," he said. "I let you. But I carved your name into my hands that night."

She swallowed. Hard.

"I want to be yours," she said, voice barely there. "If you still want me."

"You've always been mine."

And when she kissed him this time—slow, deep, and ruined— it wasn't desperation anymore.

It was a promise.

# 7

MORGAN

The bed wasn't hers. But it felt like it.

Wider than the bunk. Sheets that smelled like cedar and sweat. A heavy quilt tucked up to her chin. And one warm, naked man curled behind her with an arm draped low across her waist like he didn't intend to let her leave. Not ever again.

Her body was sore. Again.

The kind of ache that came from being touched—worshiped—like she was more need than woman. Her hips still bore the imprint of his hands. Her inner thighs? Useless.

And her heart? Fucking traitorous.

She eased up onto one elbow, wincing a little, and looked around.

His boots were by the door.

Her gear was beside them.

On the counter: two mugs. The same damn tin of cocoa she found her first night.

And next to the sink?

Two toothbrushes. His. And a brand new one in a wrapper. Pink.

She swallowed hard.

Behind her, Lynx stirred.

"You're staring," he muttered, voice thick with sleep.

Her voice cracked. Soft. Small. Like something broke open and let light in.

"You bought me a toothbrush."

He shrugged behind her.

"Figured you'd need it."

"That confident, huh?"

"You came back." He pressed a kiss to her shoulder. "I'm not letting you go again."

She rolled toward him, the sheet slipping low, her breasts bare, her heart louder than it should've been.

"You gonna keep me locked up in the cabin?"

"Only if you ask real nice."

She laughed, breath catching. He kissed her again, slower this time. Surer.

"You're not a mistake," he said against her mouth. "And I'm not a kid."

"No," she whispered. "You're a fucking mountain man."

"Your mountain man."

And she knew—deep in her bones and between her thighs—she wasn't going anywhere.

HE COOKED. Bacon. Eggs. Toast that didn't burn this time.

She was in nothing but his shirt, mug in hand, watching him like he was doing something illegal with a cast iron skillet.

"You always feed your conquests?"

He turned. Smirked.

"Only the ones I want to keep."

They ate on the porch. She noticed something in the yard she hadn't before—a small hand-carved sign planted near the trailhead.

She walked over. Brushed her fingers across it.

"Morgan's Trail – Est. This Fall"

Her breath caught in her throat.

It wasn't just a joke. It wasn't temporary.

He'd marked the trail like he believed she'd come back. Like her being there wasn't a mistake—it was a beginning.

She hadn't planned to stay. She hadn't even planned to feel.

But now? The thought of leaving felt heavier than the hike in.

She hadn't fallen. She'd walked straight into something real.

"You did this?"

"Figured you might want to leave a mark."

"I already did," she said softly, "all over your back."

He grinned, slow and proud.

SHE'S WRAPPED in his flannel. Bare legs up in his lap. They're watching the trail wind down the hill. Leaves scatter like confetti. A red squirrel stashes food under her boot.

He's tracing circles on her knee.

"You ever gonna get tired of this?"

"Of what?"

"Waking up beside me. Letting me feed you. Letting me fuck you stupid in every room of this cabin."

She grins.

"Not likely."

He tugs her closer.

"Good."

Then softer. Quieter.

"I'll build whatever life you want, Morgan. Just tell me where to start."

She presses her forehead to his.

"Start right here."

She shifted in his lap, the grin turning sly. "You sure you're up for another round?"

"Woman," he said, already half-hard against her hip, "I'd crawl through fire to get to you."

She rolled her hips once—slow and playful. "Good. Because I'm not done with you either."

He groaned, low and rough, hands sliding under the flannel. "Fuck, Morgan."

"No," she whispered, brushing her mouth against his. "I want to take you. Only you."

He kissed her like the world had gone still. No hurry this time. Just heat, promise, and slow, reverent hunger.

She guided him to the floor. To the blanket. To one more chance to prove they weren't done learning each other yet.

SHE PADDED IN BAREFOOT, wearing nothing but his shirt and a sleepy smile that hit him right in the chest.

He was at the stove, flipping bacon with the confidence of a man who finally understood what it meant to cook for someone who might stay. Her coffee was already steaming on the counter. His shirt barely hit mid-thigh on her. No bra. No shame.

Perfect.

"You always cook like this?" she asked, leaning against the doorframe, mug in hand.

"Only when I want someone to feel spoiled."

She blinked. Then smiled into her cup.

He made eggs. Burned the toast just a little. She didn't care. Ate every bite like it was a damn gift.

They took their plates outside. Sat on the porch. The air was cool but not cold. The trees were just starting to turn. Leaves scattered across the trail like the mountain wanted to dress up for her too.

She nudged his leg with her bare foot.

"You really live like this? Every day?"

"Mostly."

"You like being alone?"

He looked at her—shirt loose, hair wild, bare legs tucked under her like she'd always belonged here.

"Did. Not anymore."

She looked away, cheeks pink. That was new. That was... his.

Her gaze drifted down the slope. He watched the moment it landed—where he'd staked that carved trail sign just after she left. She didn't speak. Didn't need to. Her fingers twitched around the rim of her plate like she was holding back something fierce.

She'd already seen it.

She came back.

And stayed.

That was enough.

"You okay?" he asked quietly.

She nodded, eyes still on the trail.

"I'm not leaving again."

He pulled her close, let her settle in his lap like it was the most natural thing in the world.

"Damn right you're not."

They sat that way for a long while—her legs draped over his, his hand idly tracing her thigh like he was still learning the shape of a life he never thought he could have.

"So what now?" she asked. "We spend all winter snowed in and naked?"

"Sounds like a plan."

"You ever gonna take me into town? Let me meet people?"

He laughed. "Let you? I'm counting on you doing the talking. I barely have the social energy for a squirrel."

"Fair. You're the muscle. I'm the charm."

"We make a hell of a team."

She tilted her head. "Think they'll ever believe I'm not just a cougar who seduced you in the woods?"

"They might."

He brushed his lips against her ear.

"But I'll know the truth."

"What's that?"

"You weren't the first woman I wanted. But you were the first who didn't make me feel like a placeholder. Like I could be something permanent. Something real."

"You didn't seduce me."

"No?"

"You saved me."

She'd come up here to remember who she was.

Turns out, she'd found out who she wanted to be instead.

MORGAN

She heard the truck before she saw it—crunching over gravel, engine too loud for the mountain air.

Lynx didn't flinch. Didn't look surprised. Just kept sipping his coffee like he'd known they were coming. Like he'd wanted her here when they did.

She stood up, suddenly aware of everything—bare legs, Lynx's shirt hanging loose around her, no bra, no plan.

"Shit. Do I look insane?"

He grinned. Smug bastard.

"You look like you got fucked against a tree yesterday."

"Jesus, Lynx—"

He kissed her cheek, then stepped back just as the truck pulled to a stop.

Three men climbed out—one older, crew-leader type with a beard that probably had its own backstory, one blond with a crooked smile, and a third guy who gave her an unreadable look before nodding politely.

The bearded one spoke first.

"Well, damn. We were wondering what happened to the kid."

"I'm not a kid," Lynx muttered.

They always said it like that. Kid. Rookie. Like being quiet meant being small. But Morgan? She looked at him like he was a whole goddamn mountain.

"Not anymore, clearly."

Morgan crossed her arms over her chest. Too late. The look she got from the blond said her appearance already told the whole story.

"This her?" the leader asked. "The woman who's got you grinning like an idiot every time your name comes up?"

Lynx stepped beside her, hand landing firm on her lower back. "This is Morgan."

She blinked. Waited. Expected to be dismissed, pitied, side-eyed.

But the older man just tipped his chin.

"You staying?"

She hesitated.

Then Lynx's thumb rubbed a slow circle into her hip.

"Yeah," she said. "I think I am."

The blond grinned. "Better brace yourself, Morgan. Mountain men like him don't play fair."

"Good," she said, smiling right back. "Neither do I."

## THE END

# CHRISTMAS WITH THE TRAIL-BUILDING MOUNTAIN MAN

# 1

    ——————

Hannah Bell squinted through the windshield, wipers slapping frantically at the falling snow as her little rental crawled up the forest road. A hand-drawn wooden sign reading *Bear's Hollow – Last Maintenance 1996* swung crookedly on a metal post, and she laughed under her breath.

Perfect. Exactly the kind of place you booked when your family's group chat gave you hives and your editor said, *"Write something snowy and sexy for the holidays, babe. Like the place you booked when your apartment felt too full of ghosts, and your inbox made your chest hurt."*

She followed the GPS's final directions up a winding gravel drive. The trees closed in tight, towering, and dark, their limbs heavy with snow. Her phone lost signal five miles ago. She prayed to the booking gods that the cabin had Wi-Fi and maybe a working fireplace that didn't smell like raccoon piss.

Then she saw it—the cabin.

A-frame, sturdy. Smoke curling from the chimney. Warm, golden light flickering through frosted windows. A truck in the driveway—dusty green, tires thick as tree trunks. She blinked at it. That wasn't in the photos. The listing had promised *privacy.*

She parked beside the truck and stepped out into the cold. Her boots crunched in fresh powder. Her breath puffed white as she pulled her parka tighter, grabbed her duffel, and started up the porch steps.

She didn't even knock.

She didn't have to.

Because the door opened, fast and hard, and he filled the frame like a warning.

Him.

Big. Broad. Beard down to his chest. Shoulders stretching a long-sleeved thermal that clung like sin. His eyes were a storm-grey that didn't forgive mistakes. He looked like the human version of a closed road sign.

"Can I help you?" he asked, voice gravel and disapproval.

Hannah smiled, because smiling was what she did when things got awkward.

"Hi! Yeah, um—this is Bear's Hollow, right?" She tugged her phone from her coat pocket, swiped open the email. "I'm Hannah Bell. I booked it for three nights through that rustic rental site. Peace & Pines? They said the key would be under the moose boot scraper."

His eyes narrowed. "You booked *this* cabin?"

"Yep." She nodded, ponytail bouncing. "Long drive up from Denver. But I made it before the big storm hit—"

"You shouldn't be here."

"Well, I am here," she said, holding up her confirmation screen. "So... unless you're squatting, I think we've got a problem."

He sighed. Like he'd been *this close* to peace before the world dropped a perky brunette and a blizzard on his porch.

"There's no mistake," he muttered. "It's my cabin. Always has been. But the site owner's my cousin. And an idiot."

She blinked. "So... it's double-booked?"

She glanced past him—firelight, gear, the edge of a clipboard visible under a stack of trail flags.

"You a ranger or something?"

"Trail builder," he said. "Private crew. We work on park rebuilds, storm damage, and wilderness access. My cousin manages the contracts. Mostly screws them up."

"So this is your base camp?"

"It's home. When I let it be."

He stepped aside just enough to let her see inside. A fire roared. A kettle hissed. A wool blanket draped over the couch like temptation. It was warm in there.

And cold as hell out here.

"Storm's rolling in hard," he said. "You can't drive back. Road will be gone by dark."

He didn't say *come in.*

But he didn't shut the door either.

She stepped over the threshold with a grin and said, "Don't worry. I'll keep out of your way."

HANNAH DUMPED her duffel by the door like she owned the place. Or maybe like she didn't care who did. Josh watched the bright pink bag fall over and smirked silently. She unzipped the bag, throwing in her scarf to the top.

Of course it was pink. Of course it had a sequined "H" stitched on the side.

She peeled off her parka, revealing a thick red sweater covered in sequined Christmas lights and a glittering green tree stretched tight over her chest. He looked away immediately.

Jesus Christ.

She clapped her hands, half-frozen fingers slapping together. "This place is adorable. Rustic meets serial killer, but in a cute way."

He didn't answer. Just kicked the door shut behind her and went back to the fire. Tossed another log in. Sparks jumped.

"Do you always wear sweaters that could give someone a seizure?" he asked.

Her smile widened. "Only in December."

She wandered toward the small kitchen. He watched as she opened a cupboard. Then another. Then the fridge. Poking around like she'd lived there forever. She found a tin of cocoa mix, opened it, sniffed.

"Score."

"Help yourself, why don't you."

"I'm going to. You offered me shelter from the storm, and I assume that includes hot beverages."

Josh grunted. "I didn't offer you anything."

She turned, tin in hand. "Well, that's rude. Most people at least pretend to be hospitable before they get snowed in with a total stranger."

"I'm not most people," he said. "And I didn't ask to get snowed in."

"Neither did I." She pointed the tin at him. "I came up here to write. Needed peace, quiet, and zero judgment. Figured a snowy cabin in the mountains would do it."

He stepped into the kitchen behind her. Too close. She didn't back off, though. Her head tilted as she looked up at him—smaller, yes. Softer, yes. But not scared.

"You're a writer?"

"Romance novels."

Of course. Of fucking course.

"That why you brought reindeer pajamas?"

She grinned. "You saw those?"

"I saw *everything* when you opened your suitcase like a drunk raccoon."

Her eyes flicked down. His shirt clung to his chest, damp with melted snow from his boots. Her gaze hesitated too long before she looked back up.

"Maybe I'll put them on later. For festive morale."

He turned, grabbing a mug. "Morale's fine. What we need is insulation and quiet."

She scooped cocoa into a second mug. "What *you* need is an attitude adjustment and maybe some sugar. Here." She handed it to him, handle out. "Holiday truce?"

Josh stared at her, then at the mug. Pink nails. Candy-cane earrings. A snowstorm outside and *this* inside.

He took the cocoa.

Not because he wanted it. But because she'd clearly already taken over the place.

And maybe... Maybe he didn't hate that.

WIND SLAMMED against the cabin like it had a grudge. The fire hissed, draft shifting under the door. Hannah jumped, sloshing her cocoa as the lights flickered once. Twice.

Then they went out.

Total darkness.

"Well, shit," she whispered.

Josh was already moving. He crossed the room in two long strides, barefoot, silent, sure. A match flared. Then another. The kerosene lantern near the fireplace that had just died sparked to life, casting shadows across his face and that damn torso. He looked like something carved out of stone and war.

"You got candles?" she asked, sipping from her mug like this was fine, totally normal.

"Top left drawer." He opened a cabinet, pulled out a small battery radio, clicked it on. Static. A gravel-thick weather voice cracked through: —*storm system intensifying—expect whiteout conditions until at least Thursday—*

She blinked. "Wait, *Thursday*?"

He nodded. Struck another match. "Snow's coming in fast. Roads will be buried by midnight. We're stuck."

She stared at him over her cocoa. "Josh."

"What."

"You're telling me I'm going to be trapped here..."

Her voice caught slightly, the weight of it settling in her chest. Alone. Snowed in. With a stranger who looked like he hadn't smiled in years.

"...with you... until Christmas?"

He looked at her. Just looked. And something behind his eyes shifted. Like he'd tried to swallow the thought, and it fought back.

"Apparently."

She set her cocoa down on the table and blew out a long breath. "Well, I guess we're roommates now. Do I get a chore chart, or should we just fight over who gets the bed?"

"There's one bed."

She blinked. "Was that a threat, a warning, or an invitation?"

Josh didn't answer. Instead, he grabbed a folded flannel from a peg near the fire and tossed it at her chest. She caught it on reflex. It smelled like cedar and him.

"You're shivering," he said. "Put that on before your teeth break from chattering."

Hannah stared at the shirt. Soft. Heavy. Worn. Definitely not hers. She looked up at him. Still shirtless. Still scowling.

"You know this counts as a grand romantic gesture in at least fifteen of my books."

He turned back toward the kitchen. "It's a shirt, not a proposal."

She slipped it on anyway, pulling it over her sweater. It hung loose and low on her thighs, the sleeves swallowing her hands. She looked ridiculous. She felt... warm.

Too warm.

She curled up in the oversized armchair near the fire. He watched her from the corner of his eye, then flicked off the lantern and let the firelight do its job.

"You need anything else?" he asked, voice lower.

"Yeah." She yawned, settling deeper into the chair. "Maybe a playlist of grunts translated into actual words."

He snorted. The first real sound from him that wasn't a bark or a sigh.

Progress.

# 2

Hannah woke to silence.

No traffic. No phones buzzing. No neighbors yelling at their kids through paper-thin walls. Just the crackle of a fire and the slow, steady breath of a man who clearly hadn't had a houseguest in years.

She stretched on the couch, flannel shirt still wrapped around her like a blanket of safety and temptation. Josh wasn't in sight, but a faint clatter from the kitchen told her he was already up, probably brooding into a mug and sharpening knives just to keep the mood festive.

She padded into the kitchen barefoot. His trucker boots sat by the door, dusted with new snow. The world outside the window was white. Like a snow globe someone had shaken too hard and left on the shelf to settle.

Josh stood at the counter, back to her, shirtless.

Because of course he was.

Muscles shifted under his skin like they had purpose. Like they were used to carrying things—packs, logs, burdens. His hair was wet from the snow. His coffee mug steamed. He hadn't heard her come in.

She cleared her throat. "Morning."

He didn't jump. Just looked over his shoulder, lifted his chin. "You sleep?"

"Like a rock. Or a girl in a cozy horror movie cabin where the killer's hot and grumpy and makes great cocoa."

Josh sipped his coffee. Said nothing.

She opened a cabinet. Then another. Found a cast iron pan and held it like a trophy.

"I'm gonna make breakfast," she declared.

Josh's brow ticked. "You cook?"

"I try. And I *own* at breakfast. C'mon, you don't want to cook for me forever, do you?"

"I never said I—"

She opened the fridge. Eggs. Milk. Bacon. God bless survivalist stockpiling.

Ten minutes later, the smoke detector screamed.

Josh crossed the room fast, grabbed the pan off the burner, and dumped it in the sink with a hiss.

"Jesus," he muttered.

"I think the bacon wanted to fight me."

He opened the window to air out the smoke. "It won."

She laughed, arms crossed, wearing his shirt, her cheeks pink from the heat and humiliation. "Okay, so maybe I don't *own* breakfast. But I tried. Doesn't that count for something?"

Josh turned, leaned against the counter. Looked her over slowly—bare feet, flushed skin, her curves wrapped in flannel and mischief. Something in his jaw flexed.

"You shouldn't be here," he said again. But this time, it didn't sound like a warning. It sounded like a reminder. To himself.

"I know," she said. "But I am."

And she smiled like she wasn't going anywhere.

She waited until he disappeared into the other room, then dropped into the oversized armchair and pulled out her phone. No bars. No Wi-Fi. Nothing but her own ridiculous optimism and a front-facing camera.

She opened the voice memo app. Hit record.

"Hey. So. I may have made a tiny tactical error."

She glanced around the cabin—firelight flickering, his flannel still draped over her knees, silence pressing softly at the edges.

"Remember how I said I was going to that snowy cabin in the woods to escape deadlines and find my creative flow? Yeah, well. It's been less peaceful retreat and more forced proximity with a broody survivalist who looks like a Viking lumberjack with a scowl addiction."

She paused, then added, "If I survive, this is definitely my next book. Although I may have to tone him down so readers don't think I made him up."

Her thumb hovered over the stop button.

"He made me cocoa. Didn't say a word. Just handed it to me like it meant nothing. But it kind of meant everything."

She hit stop. Saved it. Tucked the phone away.

No signal. Still.

But honestly? That was starting to feel like a gift.

AFTER THE BACON disaster and a half-hearted attempt at scrambled eggs that looked like regret, Hannah gave up on cooking and wandered the cabin while Josh went outside to clear snow from the porch.

She wandered the cabin, trailing her fingers over the wood grain and well-worn edges of the furniture. Everything in here had a place. A purpose.

The logs weren't perfect—they creaked when the wind hit right—but the warmth they held had soaked deep, like the bones of the place remembered every fire ever lit.

It made her think about her own place—or lack of one. She'd moved apartments three times in four years, always chasing quiet, never finding peace. Deadlines, contracts, book tours... none of it ever settled her the way this silence did.

What would it feel like to stop running?

She exhaled and kept moving, eyes tracing the space as she went. She'd expected bare bones—maybe some moose antlers, dusty taxidermy, a sad couch. Instead, the place felt lived-in. Clean. Minimal. But there were details that told stories: the sharp organization of his tools, the stack of worn paperbacks by the fireplace, the carefully folded wool blankets in a crate by the hearth.

One book sat separate on a shelf. She pulled it down.

Field Engineering Manual – U.S. Army Corps. A name inside the cover in blocky handwriting: *J. Callahan.*

She flipped through it, and halfway in, tucked between two pages, she found a photograph.

He was younger. Clean-shaven, almost. Army fatigues. Arms crossed. Eyes still sharp, still distant. Next to him stood another man, smiling wide, arm slung over Josh's shoulder like they'd been through hell and come back tighter for it.

Her fingers brushed the corner of the photo. It wasn't posed. It was personal.

Josh's voice came from behind her like a blade.

"Don't touch that."

She jumped, heart slamming.

He stood just inside the door, boots off, arms crossed. Snow in his hair. A flush in his jaw that had nothing to do with cold.

"I wasn't snooping. I was—"

"You were *looking*. Same thing."

She slid the photo back into the book and set it down, slow and careful. "Sorry. I didn't mean to dig."

His glare didn't soften. "You got questions?"

Hannah met his eyes. "Who's the guy next to you?"

Josh stared at her. Long enough she almost apologized again. Then he said, voice low, "Staff Sergeant Tyler Grant. Afghanistan. Died five years ago."

The words landed heavy. Final. Like granite dropped on a glass floor.

She swallowed. "He looks like he was your friend."

Josh looked away. "He was my shadow. My balance. The dumbass who never missed a Christmas."

She didn't answer. Didn't move. She wasn't sure if reaching out would help or get her shut out completely.

"I get it," she said finally. "People have ghosts. Mine show up in texts from relatives I can't stand and edits I don't want to do. Yours live in a cabin that doesn't forgive curiosity."

He looked at her again. Slower this time. Not soft. But not armored, either.

"You ask a lot of questions."

"I'm a writer. It's in the job description."

Josh stepped past her, grabbed the book, and tucked it back on the shelf without looking at it. Then he said, almost grudgingly, "Thanks for not dropping it."

"Thanks for not throwing me out yet."

He snorted. "Not like I've got a choice."

"Oh, I don't know," she said, curling back into the chair by the fire. "I think you're warming up to me."

He grunted. But he didn't deny it.

# 3

The fire crackled low, shadows dancing across rough log walls. Josh sat in the armchair with his legs stretched out, his long body sprawled like he owned the entire damn mountain—and maybe he did.

Hannah curled on the couch, a blanket pulled to her chin, his flannel shirt still draped over her like a claim. She'd stopped trying to fill the silence with conversation. He wasn't biting. Just sat there sipping whiskey, watching the flames like they owed him money.

So she picked up her Kindle, opened her current read, and cleared her throat dramatically.

Josh didn't look up.

"Chapter twelve," she announced, loud and bright. "Her thighs trembled as he growled into her skin—*mine. Only mine.*"

He still didn't look at her. But she saw it—the way his jaw tightened, how his grip on the glass flexed.

"His fingers slid beneath the hem of her sweater, callused and rough, coaxing a gasp from her lips..."

She paused. Looked over the top of the Kindle. "Want me to stop?"

He stared at the fire like it was his only friend.

"Free country," he muttered.

She smiled. Kept reading.

"Her body arched under his touch, desperate, aching. She was soft everywhere. He was hard *everywhere*."

Josh shifted in his chair. Just a little. But enough to notice.

"You okay over there?" she asked sweetly.

He finally looked at her. His eyes locked on hers, heat dark and deliberate. "You really read that shit?"

"Professionally," she said. "But yeah. Sometimes it's the only thing that warms me up."

His eyes dropped, just for a second. Her legs were tucked under her, bare calves peeking out from under the blanket. Her hair was down now, wild and messy. Her lips were parted.

Josh drained the last of his whiskey and stood.

Hannah blinked. "Where are you going?"

He walked past her toward the kitchen, voice low and tight. "Getting another drink. Before I decide to show you what real warming up feels like."

She froze.

He didn't look back.

She stared at the fire, heart thudding, blood hot. That wasn't a joke. That wasn't banter. That was a warning.

Or a promise.

Maybe both.

She didn't ask. Didn't dig. Just smiled and let the silence breathe. And that... that felt safer than any therapy session ever had.

And she wasn't entirely sure which one she wanted more.

OUTSIDE, the night curled quiet around them, a hush broken only by the occasional creak of settling beams. The world beyond the cabin forgotten.

Josh lay on his back in the single bed, arms crossed over his chest, staring at the ceiling like it had answers. He could still hear her voice—every word she'd read, every breath she'd taken, every shift of that goddamn blanket.

She was ten feet away on the couch.

Not asleep. He could hear that too.

The soft flutter of breath. The little rustle of her turning onto her side. Again. Again.

"Just come over here," he muttered.

Silence.

Then—

"What?"

He exhaled slow. Loud enough to be clear. "You're not sleeping. I'm not sleeping. And I'm not gonna pretend that couch is a reasonable bed for anyone over four foot eight."

Another pause. A beat of hesitation.

Then the creak of the floorboards. The blanket dragging behind her. She padded into the bedroom, wrapped in it like armor, his flannel shirt loose on her frame.

She stopped at the edge of the bed. "I snore."

"So do I."

"I steal covers."

"You try, you lose."

She laughed softly, then slipped in beside him. Not touching, but near. Close enough.

The bed creaked. The air shifted.

Her voice broke the quiet. "Josh?"

He didn't answer.

"I liked what you said earlier."

He turned his head. Her face was barely lit by the last lick of flame through the cracked door.

"What'd I say?"

"That line about warming me up."

His pulse hit harder.

"You think I was joking?" he asked, voice low.

"No," she whispered. "I think you were holding back."

A long pause.

Then she rolled, her knee brushing his thigh under the blanket, her fingers grazing the edge of his arm.

He didn't move. He didn't speak.

But he didn't stop her either.

So she whispered, "Still holding back?"

Josh rolled toward her, slow and deliberate, until the heat of him pressed against her full. His hand slid under her blanket. Cupped her hip. Gripped. He told himself he wouldn't do this. Had told himself for years that getting close was too dangerous. But she was already here—inside his bed, inside his quiet, inside his goddamn chest.

"I was trying to be decent," he growled. "That's not gonna last."

Not when she looked at him like that. Like she saw the cracks and wanted to kiss them anyway. Like he was more than just what he'd lost.

He hesitated. Not because he didn't want her—but because he did. Too much. Enough that it scared him.

Touch her, and this becomes real. Not just heat. Not just a night.

But she didn't flinch. And neither did whatever was left of the man he'd tried to bury under snow and silence.

Josh's hand tightened on her hip. He didn't move fast. He moved deliberate, like he'd been holding this back so long it hurt.

"Josh..."

He growled low, mouth sliding down her throat. "You smell like cocoa and trouble."

She arched into him, one leg sliding between his. He shifted, pinning her beneath him in one hard, perfect motion. His body blanketed hers. Big. Hot. Inescapable.

She moaned. "God, you're—"

"Built for this?" he muttered, teeth grazing her collarbone.

She laughed. "Full of yourself much?"

"I've been full of restraint for two damn days." His hand gripped her thigh. "You climb into my bed wearing my shirt and read me filth like it's foreplay. What'd you think was gonna happen?"

"I was hoping for exactly this."

He kissed her . Lingering, deliberate. Like he needed to map every curve of her mouth and never forget it. His hips pressed against hers, hard and ready.

She could feel everything.

He broke the kiss long enough to whisper against her lips, "Say the word, sunshine. One word and I'll stop."

Her answer came fast, breathless, eager.

"Don't."

JOSH KISSED her like he was trying to relearn how. Like she was something he hadn't tasted in years—hope, heat, hunger that didn't come with guilt.

His hand slid beneath her sweater, up over soft skin and curves he hadn't earned but couldn't stop touching. She was warm and pliant beneath him, her breath hitching every time his fingers grazed something new.

She tugged at his shirt.

He let her.

She pushed it up over his chest, palms splaying against muscle and scars, brushing that tight line of hair that vanished under the waistband of his flannel pants.

"God," she whispered, "you're really built for this."

He smirked against her mouth. He kissed her again. Deeper. Slower. His thigh pressed between hers, opening her. She arched against him, nails raking down his back.

His hands slid down, hooking under the backs of her knees. He pulled her against him, hips grinding once—rough, hungry, unfiltered.

She gasped. "Josh..."

He reached for her panties, tugged them down her thighs but stopped just before taking them off completely. Breathing heavy. Staring at her.

"Hannah," he said, voice hoarse. "This isn't just sex."

She blinked. "No shit."

He sat back on his heels, looking down at her. Her hair fanned over his pillow, skin flushed, lips swollen, shirt unbuttoned half-way, and barely hanging on.

"I've spent the last five years avoiding everyone. Especially women who smile like they believe in things."

Her chest rose and fell. "So don't believe in me. Just... touch me."

Josh stared for another breath. Then another.

And then he kissed her like he'd decided she was the only real thing left in the world.

# 4

H annah straddled him.

Not shy. Not hesitant. Legs spread wide over his lap, thighs flushed, eyes locked on his like she was daring him to stop her.

Josh didn't breathe. He couldn't. Not when her hands were on his chest, her hips hovering, the last barrier of cotton sliding between them.

The flannel shirt hung open. Her skin was bare underneath.

She was curves and heat and everything he'd tried to live without.

His gaze dropped. Full breasts, flushed and heavy, nipples peaked like they ached for his mouth. He nearly groaned just looking at them.

"You sure about this?" he asked, voice rougher than gravel.

She rocked once. Just enough to make him curse under his breath.

"Fuck, sunshine... you're already soaked."

"If I wasn't, I wouldn't be naked in your lap, cowboy."

His hands gripped her thighs. "I'm not a cowboy."

She rolled her hips again, slow and grinding. His head dropped back against the pillow.

"Jesus—you ride like you were made for it."

"You are tonight," she whispered.

He grabbed her waist. Lifted her just enough to position himself, then paused.

"This isn't gonna be slow," he warned.

"Then don't make it slow."

He thrust up as she sank down, and everything else disappeared.

She gasped as he filled her, the stretch sharp, perfect, addictive. Her head fell back, body arching as she took all of him.

No storm. No past. No ghosts.

Just heat. Tight and wet around him. Her nails in his shoulders. Her breath ragged and wild in his ear.

Her thighs clenched around his hips, trapping him. Her breasts bounced with every thrust, mouth parted, begging for more.

Josh groaned, hands bruising on her hips, dragging her down again and again. Every thrust felt like breaking something open. Not just the hunger. The fear. The years of cold he'd wrapped around himself to feel safe.

"You feel—" he grunted, "—so damn good."

"Fucking heaven, Hannah. You grip me like you don't wanna let go."

She whimpered. "Don't stop. Please, Josh—don't stop."

He flipped her, rolled them over in a single motion, pressing her into the mattress with his weight, his mouth on her throat, his hips pounding now. Harder. Deeper.

"Take it. You wanted it fast—now take all of it."

"I told you I'd warm you up," he growled.

She shattered under him, legs shaking, fingers clawing at his back. Her body clenched around him, dragging him over the edge with a broken curse and a kiss that felt like surrender.

He cursed into her neck, voice raw, body shaking as he emptied into her like he couldn't hold anything back.

When it was over, he didn't move.

He stayed inside her. Stayed close.

Like maybe if he didn't let go, the world wouldn't come crashing back in.

Her hands slid over his back, slow, almost lazy. She traced a scar near his right shoulder blade, then another at his waist.

"You've been through it," she murmured.

"Still standing."

She kissed his chest, right over the heartbeat still hammering for her.

"Built strong," she whispered. "Built for me."

And maybe, she realized, she was tired of being built for temporary things.

Short deadlines. Fast flights. Disposable apartments. Relationships that fizzled before the second cup of coffee.

Josh didn't just make her feel wanted—he made her want something real. And that scared her more than any blank page ever had.

JOSH WOKE to the scent of her.

Warm skin. Vanilla. Cocoa and something deeper—something that didn't come from any bottle. The kind of scent that lingered in sheets and stayed in your lungs long after the woman was gone.

Only this time, she hadn't left.

Hannah lay curled against him, her leg draped over his hip like she belonged there. The light outside the window was soft, gray with snow still falling. A quiet kind of morning.

His arm was under her, hand resting on the small of her back. Bare skin. Smooth. Real.

She stirred slightly, pressing her nose against his chest with a sleepy hum.

"You're awake," she mumbled.

"I've been awake," he said quietly.

"How long?"

"Long enough to start wondering what the hell just happened."

She looked up, eyes half-lidded, lips swollen from sleep and sex. "You made good on that whole warming-me-up threat."

His mouth twitched. "You make it hard to behave."

"I'm not interested in your good behavior, Josh."

That pulled a soft grunt from him. He leaned in, kissed her temple, lingered longer than he should have.

Her fingers drifted over his chest. "You gonna freak out now?"

"No."

"You sure?"

He looked down at her. "No."

She smiled.

He sat up slowly, dragging the covers with him, and stood to stretch. Naked, broad, beautiful in the early light. She watched him with no shame whatsoever.

"What are you doing?" she asked.

He didn't answer. Just pulled on his joggers and walked into the living room. He returned a minute later with something behind his back. He sat on the edge of the bed, handed it to her without a word.

It was a cup of coffee.

Not just any coffee—he'd made it exactly the way she had the first day. Too much creamer. A ridiculous amount of sugar. Cinnamon sprinkled on top.

She stared at it, then at him.

"You remember?"

"You said it was the only thing that made winter tolerable," he muttered, rubbing the back of his neck.

Her throat tightened. "Josh..."

"Don't get weird about it."

"I'm *going* to get weird about it. You made me my Christmas coffee."

He shook his head, eyes rolling. But he didn't pull away when she reached for his hand. Didn't flinch when she laced their fingers together.

She squeezed once.

He squeezed back.

No words. No promises.

But something shifted in that silence. Something real. Something neither of them dared name—but both knew wasn't going away.

# 5

---

Josh woke first.

Not because of nightmares or a draft, but because her foot was wedged between his calves and she was breathing against his neck. neck. They had spent the previous day in bed. Sleep had only come when they both couldn't move anymore.

Her hair was a wild snarl against his shoulder. Her arm lay heavy over his stomach. She snored, just a little. Soft. Rhythmic. It should've annoyed him.

It didn't.

He lay still for a while, watching the snow drift past the window and thinking, for maybe the first time in years, that silence didn't have to mean being alone.

When she stirred, it wasn't dramatic. Just a stretch, a sigh, a sleepy brush of her cheek against his chest.

"You still here?" she mumbled.

Josh grunted. "Barely. You're hogging the bed."

"Lies," she said, eyes still closed. "You're like a furnace with boundary issues."

"Complaining?"

"Never." Her voice was soft, warm. Real.

He shifted, kissed her forehead, then rolled out of bed. The floor was cold on his feet. Her laughter followed him into the kitchen.

Ten minutes later, she padded out wrapped in his flannel, hair in a messy knot, face flushed with sleep and something softer.

"Coffee?" he asked, already holding out her mug.

She took it. Sipped. Grimaced. "Too bitter."

He raised a brow.

She reached for the creamer and sugar. "Fixable."

She took another sip and smiled like it tasted like more than just caffeine.

He leaned back against the counter and watched her for a minute.

"What?"

"You're barefoot again," he said.

"I like feeling things," she replied. "Wood, warmth, consequences."

He snorted. "You're gonna feel consequences when your toes fall off."

"Then I guess you'll have to keep warming me up," she teased.

He didn't answer.

He just stepped forward, wrapped an arm around her waist, and kissed her slow—like the night before wasn't over yet.

And maybe it wasn't.

Maybe it was just beginning.

HANNAH ZIPPED HER DUFFEL.

The sound was too loud in the quiet cabin. Like a door slamming in her chest.

She hadn't meant to fall for him. She'd come up here to breathe, to hide, to write something sexy and easy and disposable.

But Josh Callahan wasn't disposable. He was difficult and scarred and silent—but not hollow.

She stepped onto the porch, bag slung over her shoulder. Snow crunched beneath her boots. The truck was half-dug out. The road? Barely visible.

The sky had begun to clear, pink streaks bruising the clouds.

She could go. She could get out before this hurt more. Before she begged him to see her and got nothing but silence in return.

Her breath fogged in front of her. She stared at the trail of boot prints in the snow.

Then she turned.

Not toward the road.

Toward the hearth. The firelight flickering through frosted glass.

She couldn't leave without saying goodbye.

Couldn't leave without looking one more time at the man who kissed her like he wanted forever and acted like he'd never have it.

She stepped back inside. Set the bag by the door.

And that's when she saw the ornament box.

She stood, stretching. Her thighs ached—tender, spent, and sore in the best kind of way.

No dramatics. No slamming drawers or throwing things. Just methodical folding and stuffing. Flannel shirt off. Jeans on. Sweater. Socks. Dignity.

Josh hadn't said a word since she walked out of that bedroom, and Hannah had no intention of chasing after a man who wanted his silence more than he wanted her.

She went over to the fireplace and saw it—a wooden crate tucked beneath the bottom shelf.

Plain pine, sanded smooth. The lid slightly ajar.

She opened it.

Inside were ornaments. Not the cheap kind. Hand-carved, simple, beautiful. Smooth circles and stars. A few initials. A small wooden bear. A heart.

Then she saw it.

A round disc. Edges singed for rustic effect. Letters etched into the wood by hand, burned in with a hot blade or wire.

*T.G. Dec. 25, 2019*

Her fingers hovered over it. She didn't have to guess. T.G.—Tyler Grant. The soldier in the photo. The ghost in Josh's eyes.

She lifted it gently. The back was plain, except for one word scratched so deep it looked like it hurt to write:

*Sorry.*

Her breath hitched.

Josh had never said who he blamed for Tyler's death. But this... this said everything.

He blamed himself.

She sat back on her heels, ornament clutched in her palm, pulse thudding hard behind her ribs.

No wonder he didn't do holidays. No wonder he kissed her like she'd disappear. Because he thought every time he let someone close, they got hurt.

Her throat tightened. Her chest ached.

Because now she *understood.*

And now—she didn't want to leave.

Not until he knew he didn't have to carry that pain alone anymore.

JOSH SAT ON THE PORCH, snow falling like static around him, cold soaking into his flannel as he stared into the trees in the backyard and tried to feel nothing.

The first winter out here, he hadn't even bothered with a tree. Just chopped wood, drank cheap whiskey, and tried to remember how to breathe without hearing Tyler's laugh bounce off every goddamn wall. The cabin felt too quiet then. Too hollow. Like a shell of a life he didn't deserve to keep.

He'd carved that ornament in a storm not unlike this one. Alone. Drunk. Fingers raw and bleeding where the blade slipped. He didn't even know who he'd made it for. Tyler? Himself? The ghost in between? It hadn't been forgiveness. Just motion. A way to bleed something that didn't show up on the skin.

He'd buried it in the crate because he couldn't bear to look at it. And he couldn't throw it away either.

Now it sat in her hands. He could see her through the window holding it like it was something precious.

He couldn't stand the sight and what it did to his heart. And that terrified him more than the grief ever had.

The cabin door creaked open behind him.

He didn't turn.

Her footsteps crunched. Slow. Steady. Then the weight of her presence beside him—*he felt it* before she even spoke.

"You could've just said the truth," she said quietly.

"I did," he muttered.

"No," she said, firmer now. "You said it was sex. That you're not built for more. That you don't do holidays or hope or connection."

He said nothing.

"But you lied, Josh."

That made him look.

She held something out in her hand.

**The ornament.**

Wooden. Scarred. **T.G. Dec. 25, 2019.** That damn word burned into the back.

*Sorry.*

He swallowed, but it scraped going down.

He looked away again.

"I get it now," she said, soft but fierce. "You lost someone. Someone important. And now you think letting anyone close is a risk. That if you care too much, they'll be taken too. So you punish yourself. You isolate. You keep your hands busy and your mouth shut and think it makes you strong."

She paused. "It doesn't. It makes you *alone.*"

He stared at the trees. Couldn't speak.

Hannah moved in front of him, forcing him to see her.

"I'm not asking you to fix me. Or yourself. I'm not trying to change your past or pretend like this is some magical holiday healing crap."

He looked at her then. Really looked.

"But I see you," she said. "I see the man who saved me from a snowstorm, who made me coffee the way I like it, who holds me like he's afraid he'll break me and wants me anyway."

Her voice dropped. "And I want you too."

His throat tightened.

"And yeah," she added, eyes glinting, "I do believe in stupid things like timing and second chances and Christmas miracles."

She placed the ornament in his hand and wrapped his fingers around it.

"Don't throw this one away."

She stood. Turned to walk back inside.

Josh stared at the ornament in his palm.

Burned.

Simple.

Heavy.

Then he looked at her.

And for the first time in five years—**he wanted to follow.**

# 6

Hannah stood at the tiny kitchen counter, hands wrapped around the mug she hadn't sipped from. The coffee had gone cold. She hadn't moved.

Not after that.

Not after handing him her heart disguised as a damn ornament.

She should've walked away for real this time. But something in her gut—something *stupid and stubborn and full of hope*—kept her frozen.

The cabin door creaked open.

She didn't turn.

Boots moved across the floor.

Still didn't turn.

Then—warmth. Behind her. His breath at her shoulder. Close enough that she could feel it stir the hair at her neck.

"I carved that the winter after Tyler died," he said quietly. "The first Christmas I spent out here."

She closed her eyes.

"I don't know if I was saying sorry to him. Or to me."

"You don't owe either of you that," she whispered.

"I owe *you* something."

He stepped back. The loss of his heat made her blink.

"Come here," he said.

She turned. He stood in the living room, beside the fireplace, his big frame awkward, his hands fidgeting like a man two seconds from bolting.

On the rug sat a wooden box.

Small. Hand-carved. Sanded smooth.

He nudged it with his boot. "Open it."

She crouched down. Flipped the latch.

Inside was a book.

A blank leather journal.

The first page held a single sentence, scrawled in ink.

*Stay.*

Her breath hitched.

He cleared his throat. "You said you came here to write. So... write."

She looked up at him.

He wasn't smiling.

He wasn't pleading.

But his hands were fists and his heart was in his eyes, raw and wide open.

"Stay," he said again, voice lower now. "Write your book. Burn the pancakes. Talk too much. Sleep in my bed. Be here."

She stood slowly, journal clutched to her chest.

Part of her wanted to say no. To pack up, to run like she always did when things got too still. But this time... it felt different.

Like maybe she was done treating her life like a series of layovers.

"Are you sure?" she asked.

"No," he said, stepping in close. "But I'm tired of pretending I don't want to find out."

She reached for him, and this time—he reached back.

JOSH KISSED her like he'd never get the chance again.

Not rough this time. Not driven by guilt or hunger or the storm outside. This was slow. Purposeful. Like every touch was a question and every sigh from her mouth was permission.

She curled her fingers into his shirt, pulled him closer. His hands moved to her waist, her hips, memorizing the shape of her. He didn't push—he held. Anchored.

"You always touch like this?" she whispered.

"Only with you," he said.

She dropped her fingers under his shirt. "You sure?" he asked, voice hoarse.

Her answer came in the form of her lips trailing from his jaw to his throat, her breath hot, her words whispered against skin.

"Yes."

"Then let me take care of you first."

Her breath caught. "Josh..."

"Lie back. Just feel."

He scooped her into his arms, carried her to the bed with a quiet reverence that made her chest ache.

No rush. No teasing.

Just need.

He laid her down, undressed her one layer at a time. His flannel. Her sweater. The shirt she'd stolen and the leggings she hadn't expected to wear under his gaze.

Her panties were damp. He kissed the inside of her knee and groaned softly. "You're already aching for it."

He kissed the curve of her stomach, the inside of her thigh, the dip at her collarbone. Then lower. Between her legs. His tongue was slow, reverent, and hungry. She gasped and arched, one hand in his hair, the other gripping the sheet.

"That's it," he murmured. "Let me hear you."

She came on his mouth, soft and sudden, with a cry that broke the silence in all the right ways. And when she gasped, when she whispered his name like it was fragile and meant to be protected —he answered her with his hands.

With his mouth.

With everything he had.

Their bodies moved in sync. No frantic heat, no wild clawing.

Just pressure. Rhythm. Connection.

When he finally pushed into her, slow and steady, her fingers laced with his, pulling him deeper. She hooked her heels at the base of his spine, holding him tight—like letting go wasn't an option.

"You fit me," she whispered, voice trembling.

"You were made for me," he said, and meant every word.

And she was.

Completely.

They moved together like they'd done this a hundred times and never once gotten it right until now.

She kissed his temple as he whispered broken things into her shoulder—things he'd never say again but meant with every ounce of his ruined heart.

"You feel like peace."

"You feel like mine."

She came with a cry, thighs trembling, nails digging into his back. And he followed—deep, hard, and quiet, like he didn't want to scare the moment away.

Afterward, he didn't move.

She didn't let him.

They stayed wrapped together under the old quilt as snow blanketed the mountains outside, and something just as heavy settled into his chest:

This wasn't just a holiday hookup.

This wasn't just a storm.

This was home.

THE FIRE HAD BURNED low again, casting only a soft amber glow across the bedroom. Josh lay on his back, one arm tucked behind his head, the other wrapped tight around the woman curled against his chest.

Hannah traced a line over his ribs with her fingertip. Barely there. Like she wasn't trying to tease—just remember.

"You always sleep with a death grip on people?" she asked softly.

"You always talk this much after sex?"

She smirked into his skin. "Not always. But the man who just made me forget my name for five straight minutes kind of earned it."

His chest rumbled with a quiet laugh. Then silence. Not cold. Not awkward. Just still.

Until she said, "I'm scared."

His head turned. "Of what?"

"That if I stay, it won't last."

Josh stared up at the ceiling. "I'm scared you'll go."

"I was planning to," she admitted. "Before."

He exhaled slowly, fingers trailing over the slope of her spine. "What changed?"

"You."

She shifted, resting her chin on his chest, looking up at him with those unguarded eyes that saw straight through the shit he used to keep people out.

"You're not who you think you are," she whispered. "You're not broken. You're just... still hurting. And I'm not here to fix that."

She reached up and touched his cheek. "I'm here to *be* with you. If you want me."

Josh caught her hand. Held it there, against his jaw.

"I want you," he said. "More than I've wanted anything in years."

The words hit harder than he expected. Made his chest feel too tight. His throat raw.

"I don't know how to do this," he added. "Any of it. But I want to try."

She ran her fingers along his chest, the muscle beneath scarred and solid. Her hand drifted lower, playful now, but slow.

"You're doing just fine so far."

His eyes darkened. "Keep touching me like that and I'm gonna do even better."

She laughed but kept touching him. "You don't have to be perfect," she said after a moment. "You just have to show up."

His voice dropped low. "I'm here, sunshine."

She smiled, wide and soft and real. "Good. Then we're already halfway there."

Josh leaned in and kissed her—slow, sure, sweet.

And in that kiss was the unspoken vow neither of them had dared say out loud yet.

Stay. Try. Want. Choose. Together.

HANNAH SLEPT TANGLED in the quilt, bare shoulder peeking out, hair spilling across the pillow like ink on a page he never wanted to stop reading.

Josh sat on the edge of the bed, shirtless, jeans half-buttoned, staring at her like a man who'd finally found the one thing he hadn't known he needed.

And didn't deserve.

But he had her. Here. Now.

So he got up. Quiet. Careful.

He pulled on boots, a flannel, stepped into the cold like it owed him peace. Snow fell in thick, slow flakes, softening the forest, burying the road, cleansing the air. Another storm, although not as severe as the last one.

He didn't take a flashlight. Didn't need it. The moon lit the clearing enough.

Behind the shed, he found what he needed—scrap wood, a small bench he hadn't finished building last summer, the carving tools he hadn't used since... well, since *before.*

He dragged the bench onto the porch.

Sat.

And began to carve.

Not with finesse. Not for art.

For *her.*

Letters, shallow but solid. Nothing poetic. Just real.

Then he set it near the edge of the deck, where she liked to sit with her cocoa. Her breath fogged the air, and she talked too much and looked at the trees like they were listening.

He went back inside before his fingers went numb. The fire had gone to embers. He stoked it, and undressed, then crawled into bed beside her again.

She shifted, sighing in her sleep, finding him without opening her eyes.

Josh kissed her shoulder and whispered against her skin.

"Merry Christmas, sunshine."

H annah woke alone.

The bed still warm beside her. Fire still glowing low. Snow still falling, thick and soft outside the window.

She stretched, bare toes curling in the blanket, his flannel shirt wrapped tight around her like it belonged to her now—and maybe it did.

She padded into the kitchen. No coffee yet. No boots by the door. Just quiet. Peaceful. A quiet that no longer echoed—just settled, like breath after laughter.

She opened the door and stepped out onto the porch barefoot.

The snow was fresh, untouched.

Except for the bench.

It sat at the far end, positioned perfectly for the view. She hadn't seen it there before. Not finished, maybe. Not until now.

Her breath caught as she stepped closer.

Three words, carved deep into the seat, rough-edged but unmistakable.

*Stay with me.*

No flourish. No grand speech. Just hands and effort and truth.

Hannah sank onto the bench, fingers brushing the letters. She smiled, lips trembling with it, chest tight and warm and full.

Behind her, the door creaked open.

Josh stood barefoot in sweats and a thermal shirt, coffee mug in one hand, beard still wild, hair a mess.

"You like it?" he asked, voice rough with sleep.

She looked back at him. "You carved a bench."

"You needed somewhere to put your coffee."

Josh walked over, set the mug beside her, and pulled her into his lap like he didn't care about the cold or the snow or anything else but *this.*

She curled into him without hesitation.

"You mean it?" she whispered.

His lips brushed her temple. "I've never meant anything more."

And she believed him.

THEY SAT TOGETHER on the porch bench, the snow still falling, the world hushed and white like it was holding its breath for them.

Josh hadn't let go of her since she'd read those three carved words. His arm around her waist, her legs draped over his lap, her head tucked under his chin.

He could've stayed like that forever.

But he had more to say.

"I've got enough in savings to take the winter off," he said quietly. "Thought I'd do some repairs around here. Maybe finish that shed. Replace the stove."

She tilted her head to look up at him. "You offering me a tour of your improvement plans or trying to talk me into sticking around long enough to play house?"

He met her eyes, serious and raw. "I'm saying I want you to be here. With me. As long as you'll have me."

Her smile softened. "I have deadlines. A life. Friends who'll panic when I tell them I'm shacking up with a mountain man who grunts more than he talks."

"I can grunt over video calls too."

She laughed.

"I don't have a ring," he added. "Yet."

Her breath caught.

"But I've got hands," he said, lifting one, "and time. And about a dozen more pieces of wood I can ruin trying to carve something that feels right."

"You're really doing this," she said, blinking.

"I'm really doing this."

He took her hand, threaded their fingers together.

"I'm not promising it'll be perfect. I'm not promising I won't screw up. But I'll show up every day. I'll hold you every night. And I'll carve your damn name into every stick of furniture if that's what it takes to prove I'm in this."

She kissed him.

Not frantic.

Not teasing.

Just full.

Slow. Steady. Real.

Like a promise returned.

"I'll have to go back," she murmured against his lips. "Pack up my place. Tell my landlord I'm not renewing."

Josh smiled.

"I'll be here," he said. "Flannel, firewood, and coffee just the way you like it."

"You mean my Christmas coffee?"

"Yes. A little sweet. And strong enough to keep me up all night."

She laughed again and buried her face in his neck.

The snow kept falling.

And neither of them needed anything more than what was already right there—in each other's arms.

LATER, after breakfast—burned toast and eggs she let him rescue this time—they didn't say much.

There wasn't anything left to explain.

Hannah stood at the window in his oversized flannel, sipping her second mug of coffee, her bare legs kissed by firelight. The snow had eased. Trees bowed low. The cabin sat wrapped in white like the mountain had decided to keep them a little longer.

Josh came up behind her, slid his arms around her waist, and pressed a kiss to the back of her neck.

"You warm?" he murmured.

She leaned into him. "Always. Now."

He rested his chin on her shoulder and watched the stillness with her. His hands moved slow over her belly, then settled low on her hips, palms wide and firm, holding her like she was something already his.

She didn't pull away.

She just reached one hand up, cupped the back of his neck, and smiled.

"You realize," she said softly, "you've completely ruined me for men who live within ten miles of a Starbucks."

"You'll survive."

"I might. If you keep carving me furniture and feeding me."

He kissed her cheek, grinning. "And?"

She turned in his arms and kissed him, slow and deep and sure.

"And keep loving me like this," she whispered.

Josh didn't answer.

He just held her tighter.

Outside, the storm had passed.

But inside, it had only just begun.

And neither of them wanted it to end.

Down the mountain, the crew would start back up in a week—new trail contract, new problems, new place to freeze their asses off.

Josh would be there. So would Beau.

And if the rumors were true, so would the redhead who'd once told Beau she'd bury his tools in the snow if he ever set foot on her property again.

Josh grinned into Hannah's hair.

Poor bastard didn't stand a chance.

# EPILOGUE

O ne Year Later
Snow piled high along the edges of the cabin, just like last year, but everything inside had changed.

Hannah shuffled across the warm wood floor, barefoot, a mug of cocoa in one hand and a half-eaten gingerbread man clutched in the other. Her baby bump peeked out beneath one of Josh's old Army shirts, stretched tight over her belly and tied in a knot above her hips.

The flannel pajama shorts rode low, and her swollen ankles weren't sexy—but the way Josh looked at her from the kitchen?

Like she was the center of every storm he wanted to chase.

"I told you to sit your cute ass down," he growled, flipping something golden in the pan.

"I *am* sitting. I'm just taking the scenic route to the chair."

"Bullshit." He turned off the burner and crossed the room in three strides, took her mug, and guided her down into the chair by the fire with all the care of a man handling a live grenade wrapped in velvet.

She grinned. "You're so bossy when I'm knocked up. It's hot."

"It's survival." He kissed the top of her head and handed her the cocoa back. "You're carrying my entire world in there."

She rolled her eyes, but her throat tightened. He said that a lot. And he always meant it.

The cabin looked like Christmas had exploded—pine garland, twinkle lights, a scraggly tree they'd dragged in from just beyond the trail line, and a pile of presents under it wrapped in kraft paper and tied with twine.

Josh brought her a plate stacked with pancakes and scrambled eggs, set it on her lap like she might float away if he let go too long.

"God, I love you," she murmured through a mouthful of syrup.

He kissed her temple. "Yeah. I'm a real fucking catch."

She laughed, set the plate down, and pointed to the stack of gifts. "Presents?"

He handed her the top one—badly wrapped, clearly done with duct tape and swearing.

Inside: a carved reading light holder made from twisted pine, her initials burned into the base.

Next: a thick handmade blanket in shades of green and gray.

Then: a mug that said *Writer Mama* with a heart under the text —and **his handwriting** burned into the ceramic.

"Josh..."

He reached behind the tree and pulled out a small square box, tied with red ribbon.

Her heart tripped.

He didn't kneel.

Didn't speak.

Just handed it to her.

She untied the ribbon, lifted the lid—and gasped.

Inside the box, nestled on a bed of cotton and cedar shavings, sat the smallest pair of wooden booties she'd ever seen.

Carved. Smoothed. Sanded with love and the calloused hands of a man who didn't say things unless they mattered.

Her fingers shook as she lifted them out. The detail was insane—tiny laces, a soft arch in the sole, the grain running like memory down the sides.

And tucked beneath them, folded in half, was a piece of parchment.

Josh watched her silently, jaw tight, eyes unreadable.

She unfolded the paper.

His handwriting was sharp. Deep. Heavy on the ink, like he'd pressed too hard to get it right.

*Still building a future. Still built for you. Always.*

Her heart cracked. Open. Wide. Bare.

She looked up at him, eyes full, lips trembling. "Josh…"

She hadn't written anything steamy since the baby kicked during a kissing scene and ruined the moment. But this—this was the love story worth getting right.

Josh sat beside her, shoulder to shoulder, watching her thumb the edges of the little booties.

"You still writing?" he asked, voice low.

She nodded. "Bits. When the baby isn't doing somersaults and I'm not napping like it's my job."

"You'll finish the new one?"

"Eventually. My editor's being patient. And I'm scaling the tour down next year—three cities, tops. I told them I'm not dragging my swollen ankles through TSA for anything less than five-star sheets."

Josh smirked. "Guess I better keep this fire going and make damn sure you want to come home."

She leaned into him, cocoa warming her palms. "You already

do."

He took the booties from her hand, then slowly sank to one knee. Not flashy. Not staged.

Just a big, quiet man kneeling in front of the woman he'd built a life around.

"I know I already asked you to stay," he said, voice thick. "And you did. I know we're building a kid, a life, this whole crazy thing."

She nodded, breath held tight in her chest.

"But I want every part of you. Every damn storm and every calm after. I want the mornings with your hair a mess. I want the nights when you hog the blanket and cry at commercials. I want this baby. I want more if you want more."

He took a ring box from his back pocket.

Simple silver. A narrow band. Her initials carved inside.

"I didn't want to do it the first year. I wanted to do it for *every* year."

He held it out, hand steady, heart not.

"So, sunshine—marry me?"

She didn't cry.

She *sobbed*.

Laughed through it. Nodded too fast. Bent down and kissed him before she could choke on the word yes.

He stood with her in his arms, one hand cupping her belly, the other gripping the back of her neck like he'd never let go.

"God, I love you," she whispered.

He smiled against her mouth. "I know."

She swatted his chest. "You *really* want to quote Han Solo right now?"

"Better than quoting Frosty the Snowman while I'm trying to get laid."

She laughed again, forehead to his.

"Wait 'til you see what I carved into the crib," he murmured.

Her brows rose. "What?"

He kissed her. "You'll find out."

The sun was dipping behind the ridge, casting a soft silver over the clearing. Snow fell like whispers. No wind, no noise. Just peace.

Josh sat on the porch bench—the same one he'd carved last Christmas. *Stay with me.* Hannah sat between his legs, leaned back against his chest, wrapped in a thick wool blanket and his arms. One of his hands rested over her belly, warm and wide. Protective.

She traced the letters on the bench with her fingertip. "You really didn't think I'd stay, did you?"

"I wanted you to," he breathed. "But I didn't think I deserved it."

Her hand covered his. "You built this whole life for me."

"No," he said, pressing a kiss to her temple. "*We* built it. You just reminded me it was worth building."

They sat in silence after that. A silence that didn't need filling. Everything worth saying was already understood.

A kick fluttered under his palm.

Josh froze.

She stilled, too.

Then it came again—stronger this time. He drew in a shaky breath. "That was real."

Hannah's eyes shone. "Told you."

Josh let both hands rest over her belly now, wide palms spanning the curve like he could anchor her—and whatever was growing inside—just by holding on.

"That's our kid," he whispered, voice thick. "I felt them."

He shook his head once, slow and reverent. "I thought the best part of my life was behind me. That I'd missed my shot."

He moved his forehead to her belly like it was sacred.

"But you, little one... you changed the ending. We weren't built to break. We were built for the storm."

Hannah wiped her eyes, swallowed the lump in her throat, and ran her fingers through his hair.

"I don't think I've ever loved anyone the way I love you," she whispered.

Josh looked up at her.

"You haven't even *seen* the crib yet," he said.

She laughed, shaky and sweet.

He pulled her closer. Wrapped her tight in his arms, blanket cocooning them both from the cold.

She peeked inside, hand to her mouth. Carved across the headboard in careful, sloping letters: *Built for you. Always.*

And beneath it, smaller—near the base rail—one more word, tucked in like a secret between them: *Sunshine.*

Flakes drifted down like the mountain was wrapping them in quiet. Nothing moved but the warmth between them.

And the storm that had started it all? It wasn't a threat anymore. It was a memory. One that had brought them home.

THE END

# CHRISTMAS VOWS FOR THE MOUNTAIN MAN

A FAKE MARIAGE CHRISTMAS ROMANCE

# 1

---

# THE CLAUSE

CLARA
I knew my aunt's will reading wasn't going to be easy; I just never assumed it would change my life.

Henderson adjusted his glasses. "Marriage by Christmas or the property reverts to the state."

There it was. Forty acres of mountain land held hostage by my dead aunt's romantic delusions. The cabin where I'd spent every summer as a kid. The barn where I planned to build my veterinary practice. All of it gone unless I found a husband in three weeks.

"Who the hell writes this crap?" I snapped. "Fake marriage for land? What is this, a Hallmark fever dream?"

Henderson cleared his throat. "Mrs. Chen was quite specific about—"

"Aunt Mae was a romance novelist with boundary issues." I stood up so fast my chair scraped against the floor. "This is insane."

But insane or not, it was legal. Ironclad. And I was screwed.

I grabbed my purse and headed for the door, Henderson's voice following me about taking time to consider my options.

What options? I could barely get a second date, let alone a marriage proposal.

The December air hit me like a slap. Christmas lights mocked me from every storefront, and my hands shook as I fumbled for my phone.

David's number was still in my contacts. We'd dated for eight months last year before he decided I "worked too much and smelled like dogs." But desperate times called for desperate ex-boyfriends.

"Clara?" His voice was cautious when he picked up. "This is unexpected."

"Hi." I tried to sound casual instead of completely unhinged. "How are you?"

"Good. Engaged, actually. Spring wedding."

I hung up without another word.

Of course he was engaged. Probably to some woman who worked normal hours and smelled like vanilla instead of antiseptic.

I scrolled through more contacts. Jake—married with twins. Mark—moved to Seattle. Tom—gay and blissfully happy with his boyfriend.

One by one, every possibility crumbled.

My back hit the brick wall, and I slid down until I was sitting on the cold sidewalk. This was it. I was going to lose everything because I couldn't find a man desperate enough to marry me in three weeks.

The tears came hot and angry. I pressed my face against my knees and let myself fall apart right there on Main Street.

A shadow fell across me.

"You all right?"

The voice was deep, rough, with quiet authority that made me look up without thinking.

Work boots. Scuffed leather, steel toes. My gaze traveled up—worn jeans that hugged strong thighs, a flannel shirt rolled to reveal forearms that could probably snap me in half. Broad shoulders that looked like they carried heavy things without complaint.

Then I saw his face.

Dark hair, storm-gray eyes, a jaw that could cut glass. He was holding rebar in one hand and a toolbox in the other, like he'd been walking past when he spotted my side walk breakdown. His mouth was set in a hard line, but his eyes weren't unkind.

They were also looking at me like he could see straight through my defenses.

"I'm fine," I lied, wiping my eyes.

"You don't look fine."

Something about the way he said it—matter-of-fact, no judgment—made my throat tight again. It also made me notice the way his voice rumbled low in his chest.

"Bad day," I managed.

"Figured." He shifted the rebar, and I caught sight of his hands. Big, scarred, callused. The kind that knew how to fix things. "You need help?"

I almost laughed. "Actually, you wouldn't happen to know anyone who wants to get married, would you?"

The words hung between us like a dare. His eyebrows went up a fraction, and I realized how insane I sounded.

"Sorry," I said quickly, scrambling to my feet. "I'm not usually this crazy. Just a really, really bad day."

He was quiet for a long moment, those storm-gray eyes never leaving my face. When they dropped to my mouth for just a second, something hot flicked through my stomach.

"Depends on the timeline," he said.

I stared at him. "What?"

"You asked if I knew anyone who wants to get married. I'm asking about the timeline."

My heart did something strange. "Three weeks."

"Reason?"

"Inheritance clause. Marry by Christmas or lose everything that matters." The words tumbled out. "I'm a vet tech, I want to start my own practice, but I need the land. My aunt left it to me with this ridiculous marriage requirement."

He nodded like this made perfect sense. Like desperate women proposed to strangers all the time.

"I'll do it," he said.

The words hit me like a physical blow. "What?"

"I'll marry you."

I blinked at him. "You don't even know me."

"Don't need to." His mouth quirked up at one corner—not quite a smile, but close. "You're not the only one who lost something up here."

Something in his voice made me study his face more carefully. There was pain there, buried deep but still visible if you knew how to look.

"Why?" I whispered.

"Because Mae saved my sister once. Figure I owe her."

Mae. He knew my aunt. That should have been reassuring, but something about the way he said it felt like there was more to the story.

"I don't even know your name," I said.

"Eli." He shifted the toolbox and held out his right hand. "Eli Hayes."

I took his hand without thinking. His palm was warm, rough with work, completely steady. When his fingers closed around mine, that heat in my stomach spread lower.

"Clara Chen."

"Nice to meet you, Clara Chen." His grip tightened just slightly, and I caught him looking at my mouth again. "You want to get married?"

## ELI

I'd been walking past the lawyer's office when I heard the crying.

Not polite tears. The real kind. The broken kind that came from somewhere deep and desperate.

I should have kept walking. Should have minded my own business and headed to the hardware store. But something about the sound stopped me cold.

Maybe because I knew what that kind of crying meant. What it felt like when the world ripped everything important away and left you with nothing but wreckage.

So I stopped. Found her.

She was small, curvy in a way that made my hands itch. Dark hair escaping from a ponytail, scrubs that had seen better days, and mascara streaked down her cheeks. She looked like she'd been wrestling with something bigger than herself and lost.

She also looked like she needed help.

And I was good at helping. Better at that than most things these days.

"You all right?" I asked.

She looked up with brown eyes that were too bright, too wet, too full of pain. But also too fucking gorgeous for her own good.

"I'm fine," she lied.

"You don't look fine."

When she told me it was a bad day, I believed her. Bad days had a particular look, and she was wearing it like a second skin.

Then she asked if I knew anyone who wanted to get married.

Most men would have backed away. Assumed she was crazy, desperate, looking for any warm body to solve her problems.

But I heard something else in her voice. Determination. Like marriage wasn't what she wanted, but what she needed.

"Depends on the timeline," I said.

She said three weeks, and something about the way she said it —like it was a death sentence—made me stay.

Inheritance clause. Land. A future that depended on finding a husband by Christmas.

Mae Chen's niece. I should have seen it sooner—she had Mae's stubborn chin, Mae's fierce eyes when she was pissed.

Mae, who'd pulled my sister out of that creek when we were kids. Mae, who'd never asked for anything in return.

"I'll do it," I said.

The words came out before I'd really thought them through, but they felt right. And when Clara stared at me like I'd just offered to move mountains, something shifted in my chest.

She was beautiful when she was shocked. Hell, she was beautiful when she was crying. But there was something about the way she looked at me in that moment—like I might actually be worth something—that made me want to prove her right.

"You're not the only one who lost something up here," I told her. True enough. I'd lost plenty in these mountains.

"Because Mae saved my sister once. Figure I owe her."

Which was true. Caitlin was alive because of Mae. But that wasn't why I was offering to marry her niece.

I was offering because Clara Chen looked at me like I was a man instead of a broken-down former sawyer who couldn't save the people who mattered. Because she needed help, and I needed to feel useful again.

Because when she took my hand, her pulse jumped under my

thumb, and I wanted to see what other reactions I could get out of her.

"You want to get married?" I asked.

She went very still, like she was waiting for the catch. But there wasn't one. Just a woman who needed a husband and a man who had nothing better to do than help her get one.

And maybe figure out why touching her made me feel like I was waking up for the first time in three years.

## CLARA

Twenty minutes later, we were sitting across from each other at Murphy's Diner, and I was trying to process what had just happened.

I'd convinved a complete stranger to marry me. And now we were discussing it while I tried not to stare at the way his hands wrapped around his coffee mug.

Big hands. Scarred. The kind that knew how to work, how to build things, how to tear them apart if necessary.

"Ground rules," Eli said.

"Ground rules," I repeated it, hoping it would make more sense the second time.

"Marriage of convenience. Nothing more." His gray eyes met mine across the table. "We do what we need to do legally, you keep your land, then we figure out what comes next."

The practical way he laid it out should have been reassuring. Instead, it felt like disappointment settling in my chest.

"What else?" I asked.

"No expectations. This isn't about romance or feelings." He paused, and something flickered in his expression. "It's about solving a problem."

Right. Problem-solving. I could do that.

So why did this feel different?

"How long?" I asked.

"However long you need to secure the inheritance." He shrugged. "After that, annulment."

Annulment. Like it never happened.

"What about you?" I asked. "What do you get out of this?"

He was quiet for a long moment, staring into his coffee. "Peace of mind, maybe."

"Everyone needs something," I said.

His mouth quirked up. "Do they?"

"Yes. So what is it really?"

Another pause. Then: "Purpose."

The word hung between us, heavy with meaning I didn't understand. But I heard the loneliness underneath it.

"I can work with that," I said.

"Can you?"

"I'm good at giving people things to do." I took a sip of coffee, grimacing at how cold it had gotten. "What do you do for work?"

"Trail crew. Forest service contracts. Road maintenance, fire suppression."

That explained the muscles. And the hands. And the way he moved like he belonged outdoors instead of sitting in diners making impossible deals.

"Are you from around here?" I asked.

"Close enough." He drained his coffee. "You?"

"Born and raised. This place gets in your blood."

He nodded like he understood. "The mountains."

"The mountains. The people." I managed a smile. "It's home."

"And now you might lose it."

"Not if you can help it."

The certainty in his voice made my chest tight. When was the last time someone had offered to help without wanting something in return?

"We should make this official," I said. "Get the license, find someone to perform the ceremony."

"When?"

"This weekend. That gives us time to get everything in order."

"This weekend works." He pulled out an old flip phone. "I'll need your number."

We exchanged information, and it felt strangely intimate. Like we were crossing some invisible line.

"One more thing," Eli said as we stood to leave. "This stays between us. No one needs to know it's not real."

"Agreed." I held out my hand. "Partners?"

His palm was warm when it closed around mine, and he held on longer than necessary. When his thumb brushed across my knuckles, that heat in my stomach flared again.

"Partners," he said, but the way he was looking at my mouth suggested he was thinking about more than business arrangements.

We walked to the door together, and when he held it open for me, I had to brush past him to get through. The contact was brief —my shoulder against his chest—but it was enough to make my breath catch.

I glanced up, catching our reflection on the diner window. We looked like a couple. Like two people who belonged together.

He held the door. I walked through.

Just like that, I belonged to a stranger.

# 2

# THE AGREEMENT

CLARA

What the hell did I just agree to?

I sat in my truck in the clinic parking lot, engine off, staring at my phone. Eli's number was already saved in my contacts—*Eli Hayes*—like he was someone I'd known for years instead of a stranger who'd offered to marry me three hours ago.

My hands were shaking. Not from cold, but from the magnitude of what I'd just committed to. Marriage. For dirt and rotting wood. For a dream I might never build.

Except it was everything. I knew that much.

Three years away. Three years building a life in Portland that never quite fit. I'd told myself I was done with small towns and mountains and the weight of everyone knowing your business. But here I was, back for Mae's funeral, back for the will reading, staying in the Pineview Motel while I figured out what came next. Back because this place had never really let me go.

I drove to Aunt Mae's property—*my* property, if I could pull this off—and parked at the end of the dirt road. The cabin sat nestled against the treeline, logs weathered silver-gray but still solid. Still home.

I walked the perimeter first, checking the fence posts Mae had installed years ago. Some were loose, others rotted through, but the bones were good. Fixable. The barn stood about fifty yards from the cabin, red paint faded but the structure sound.

Inside the barn, hay dust danced in the late afternoon light. I breathed in the smell of old summers—sweet grass, leather, the lingering scent of the horses Mae used to board. The stalls were empty now, but I could picture them full. Could see the examination room I'd build in the corner, the surgery suite, the recovery pens for wildlife rehab.

This wasn't just land. This was my future.

I stepped into the last stall, the one Mae had never finished. The wood was raw, unstained, but sturdy. I ran my hand along the rough boards and felt something settle in my chest.

*This matters,* I told myself. *This is worth it.*

Worth marrying a stranger. Worth weeks of pretending. Worth whatever complications came with tying my life to Eli Hayes, even temporarily.

Because this place wasn't just Mae's legacy. It was mine.

I pulled out my phone and typed before I could second-guess myself:

*Can you do dinner tonight? Need to talk through details.*

The response came back almost immediately: *Address is 247 Mill Creek Road. Six o'clock work?*

No questions. No hesitation. Just practical certainty, like he'd been expecting me to follow through.

Maybe he understood better than I did that some things were worth the risk.

· · ·

## ELI

I'd been cleaning for an hour.

Not because the cabin was dirty—I kept it tidy out of habit—but because Clara Chen was coming over, and for some reason that felt like it mattered.

I folded the towels on the bathroom counter. Swept the kitchen floor. Made sure there were no empty beer bottles or dirty dishes lying around. The place was small—one bedroom, one bathroom, a living area that flowed into the kitchen—but it was mine. Had been for three years, ever since I'd bought it with my severance pay and the need to disappear.

At five-thirty, I started dinner. Grilled cheese and tomato soup, because it was simple and I didn't want to mess it up. Because something about Clara had made me want to feed her, take care of her, make sure she was warm and safe.

While the soup heated, I went to the closet and pulled down the box I'd been avoiding for months. Mae's things—the stuff she'd left behind, the items her lawyer had asked me to hold onto until Clara came back.

I'd forgotten about the flannel shirt until I saw it folded at the bottom of the box. Forest green, soft from years of wear, with *FFA* embroidered on the pocket. It had probably belonged to Clara when she was in high school.

I shook it out, checked for holes or stains. Found none. Smelled faintly of lavender and cotton. Like it remembered her.

At six-fifteen, I heard truck tires on gravel.


## CLARA

Eli's cabin was exactly what I'd expected and nothing like I'd imagined.

It sat in a clearing surrounded by pine trees, with a covered porch and windows that glowed warm yellow in the gathering dusk. Practical. Sturdy. The kind of place that could weather any storm.

But it was also beautiful in a quiet way that surprised me.

I knocked, and he opened the door before I could second-guess myself.

"Hey," he said.

"Hey."

He stepped aside and took my coat as I entered. "Come in."

I brushed past him in the doorway, caught the smell of soap and pine and something heavier underneath. Sweat. Smoke. Him.

His shirt clung to his arms. Clean flannel stretched across shoulders that looked like they could carry anything. Fresh soap. Heat underneath.

The inside was warm, neat, and surprisingly comfortable. A leather couch faced a stone fireplace. Bookshelves lined one wall, filled with what looked like technical manuals and a few paper-backs. The kitchen was small but well-organized, with copper pots hanging from hooks and herbs growing in mason jars on the windowsill.

It felt like a home, not just a place to sleep.

"Dinner's ready," Eli said. "Nothing fancy."

"I'm not fancy either."

Since it was winter and my boots were damp from the snow, I kicked them off by the door, immediately feeling smaller in my stocking feet. Eli's gaze dropped to my feet. Not long. Just enough to make me aware of every inch of skin I hadn't bothered to hide.

"Hungry?" he asked, voice rougher than before.

"Starving."

He'd set the small kitchen table for two, with actual plates and cloth napkins. The soup steamed in ceramic bowls, and the grilled cheese was cut diagonally, crispy and golden.

"This looks amazing," I said, and meant it.

"Just soup and a grilled cheese."

"Just soup and a grilled cheese that someone made for me." I sat down across from him. "When's the last time someone cooked for you?"

He was quiet for a moment. "Been a while."

I took a bite of the sandwich. Perfect—buttery bread, melted cheese, the kind of comfort food that made you forget your problems for a few minutes.

"This is really good," I said.

"Thanks."

We ate in comfortable silence for a few minutes. Then Eli got up and returned with something folded in his hands.

"Mae had me keep some things for you," he said, holding out a green flannel shirt. "This was in the box."

I recognized it immediately. My old FFA shirt from high school, the one I'd worn to every livestock show and barn cleaning. I'd wondered where it had gone.

"How did Mae have this?"

"She said to give it to you when you came back for good." He paused. "Guess she knew you would eventually."

I took the shirt, ran my fingers over the soft fabric. It still smelled faintly like the barn, like the girl I used to be before life got complicated.

"You can keep it," I said. "I don't really—"

"It's yours now," he said, and something in his voice made me look up. His gray eyes were serious, almost intense. "Everything that was Mae's is yours now."

The way he said it made my breath catch. Like he wasn't just talking about the shirt.

I slipped it on over my sweater, and it fit perfectly. Soft and worn and familiar, like coming home.

"Why did you really say yes?" I asked. "To marrying me."

His jaw worked. "Does it matter?"

"Yes."

A long beat. The fire crackled. Then: "I told you that Mae saved my sister. Pulled her out of Mill Creek when she was ten."

"That's it?"

He didn't answer. Just stared into his coffee like it held secrets he wasn't ready to share.

"What happened?" I pressed.

"To who?"

"To you. To make you willing to marry a stranger."

Something shuttered completely in his expression. "That's not part of the deal."

"Okay," I said. "You said purpose at the diner. I can give you that."

"Can you?"

"I'm good at finding things for people to do. Ask anyone."

That almost-smile tugged at his mouth. "What if I'm not good at taking orders?"

"Then we'll figure something else out."

After dinner, I helped him clean up, moving around his kitchen like we'd done this a hundred times before. When he washed, I dried. When I reached for a high cabinet, he was there to open it for me.

It felt domestic in a way that made my chest tight.

"You can stay if you want," he said when the last dish was put away. "Talk through details. Plans."

I looked toward the hallway, toward what had to be his bedroom. "Where would I sleep?"

"Couch is comfortable."

I curled up on the leather couch, pulling my legs under me. Eli sat on the other end, careful to keep space between us, but I could feel the heat from his body anyway. Could smell that mix of soap and something darker that clung to his skin.

"So," I said. "What happens next?"

"We get the license tomorrow. Find someone to perform the ceremony."

"That's it?"

"That's the legal part." He looked at me, and his eyes lingered on the flannel shirt. On the way it hung loose over my curves. His jaw flexed, like he'd just remembered this was supposed to be pretend. "What else did you have in mind?"

I didn't know. But sitting here in his warm cabin, wearing my old shirt that Mae had saved for me, watching the firelight play across his features, it felt like there should be more.

Like we were crossing a line that couldn't be uncrossed.

"Clara," he said quietly.

"Yeah?"

"You sure about this?"

I looked around his cabin—at the books on the shelves, the careful way he'd arranged everything, the photo turned face-down on the refrigerator that I was pretending not to notice.

"I'm sure," I said.

He stood then, walked toward his bedroom. Stopped in the doorway and looked back at me.

"There's a blanket in that chest if you get cold," he said.

I curled tighter in my old shirt. His eyes flicked to me once more before he disappeared into his room.

He didn't close the door. The flannel smelled like old hay and pine. Like him. And I didn't sleep.

# 3

## THE LICENSE

CLARA

The courthouse steps were slick with ice at eight-thirty in the morning.

I stood at the bottom, clutching the paperwork I'd printed at home, watching my breath cloud in the December air. The marriage license office opened at nine. Eli was supposed to meet me here at eight-forty-five.

It was eight-forty-six.

Maybe he'd changed his mind. Maybe he'd woken up and realized how insane this was—marrying a woman he'd known for less than twenty-four hours for reasons he wouldn't explain.

Maybe I'd pushed too hard last night, asking questions he wasn't ready to answer.

"You're early."

I spun around. Eli stood behind me, hands shoved deep in his jacket pockets, gray eyes unreadable in the morning light. He looked like he'd slept about as well as I had.

"So are you," I said.

"Figured we should get this done before we lost our nerve."

*We.* Like this was something we were doing together instead of a favor he was doing for me.

"You having second thoughts?" I asked.

His gaze dropped to my mouth, lingered there for a beat too long. "Are you?"

"No."

"Then let's go get married."

The marriage license office was a sterile room with fluorescent lighting and forms taped to every available surface. The clerk behind the counter looked like she'd rather be anywhere else.

"Next," she called without looking up.

We approached the counter together. Eli's hand found the small of my back, a touch so brief I might have imagined it if not for the heat that shot straight through me.

"We need a marriage license," I said.

The clerk finally looked up, took in Eli's size and my obvious nervousness, and her expression shifted to something resembling interest.

"IDs and birth certificates," she said. "You both residents of the county?"

"Yes," Eli said, pulling out his wallet.

"How long have you known each other?"

I froze. We hadn't practiced this part.

"Long enough," Eli said smoothly. His hand pressed against my back again, steadying me.

The clerk raised an eyebrow but started typing. "Previous marriages?"

"No," I said.

"No," Eli echoed.

"Witnesses for the ceremony?"

Another pause. "We'll figure that out," I said.

Twenty minutes and sixty-five dollars later, we walked out of the courthouse with a piece of paper that made our fake marriage suddenly, terrifyingly official.

"That's it?" I asked, staring at the license.

"That's it." Eli stopped on the courthouse steps. "Clara."

"Yeah?"

"We need to talk about the ceremony."

"What about it?"

His eyes were serious, almost intense. "If people show up, they're going to expect things. Rings. Vows. A kiss."

A kiss. My stomach flipped at the thought of Eli's mouth on mine, even for show.

"Right," I said. "Of course."

"You okay with that?"

Was I okay with kissing a man who made my pulse skip just by looking at me? A man whose flannel shirt I'd slept in because it smelled like him?

"It's just for show," I said.

Something flickered in his expression. "Right. Just for show."


ELI

Clara was lying.

I could tell by the way her voice went tight when she said it was just for show. By the way her cheeks flushed when I mentioned kissing her.

Good. Because I was lying too.

Nothing about this felt like pretend anymore. Not the way she'd looked curled up on my couch last night. Not the way she'd smiled when she put on her old shirt. Not the way my chest had tightened when she'd asked about my past.

And definitely not the way I wanted to kiss her for real, not just for whatever audience we'd have at our wedding.

"We should find someone to perform the ceremony," I said.

"Any suggestions?"

"Nash Morrison. He's ordained—did his brother's wedding last year."

Clara nodded. "When?"

"This Saturday, maybe."

"That fast?"

"You said you had to be married within three weeks. Better to have extra time in case something goes wrong."

What I didn't say was that I wanted it done. Wanted her legally tied to me before she could change her mind or realize she could find someone better.

I kept telling myself it was fake. Kept telling myself it didn't matter. But I was already planning forever like a fool.

We were walking toward the parking area when I heard my name called.

"Eli Hayes, is that you?"

I turned to see Dolores Finch bearing down on us, her curiosity radar clearly pinging. Dolores ran the post office and knew everyone's business before they did.

"Mrs. Finch," I said.

Her eyes went straight to Clara, then to the courthouse behind us, then back to Clara with the kind of calculating look that spelled trouble.

"And who's this lovely young lady?"

"Clara Chen," Clara said, extending her hand. "Mae Chen's niece."

"Oh, Mae's girl! Of course!" Dolores beamed. "I heard you were back in town. And at the courthouse with our Eli, no less."

I watched Clara's face carefully. This was the test—could she lie convincingly to the town gossip?

"We just got our marriage license," Clara said, and I nearly choked.

Dolores's eyes went wide. "Marriage license? Well, I'll be! When's the happy day?"

"This Saturday," Clara continued smoothly. "Small ceremony. Just family."

"How wonderful! And so romantic, getting married right before Christmas." Dolores turned to me. "Eli, you sly dog. How long have you two been—"

"We should go," I interrupted. "Lots to plan."

I put my hand on Clara's back and guided her toward her truck before Dolores could ask more questions.

"I can't believe you just did that," I said once we were out of earshot, but I was grinning.

"Was it bad?" Clara looked worried. "I just told the town gossip we're getting married on Saturday."

"It was perfect. Now we have a deadline and a story."

"Eli." She stopped walking and turned to face me. "What if people ask questions? What if they want details about how we met, how long we've been together?"

"Then we tell them it was fast. That Mae introduced us. That sometimes you know when something's right."

The words came out more intense than I'd intended. Clara stared at me, something shifting in her expression.

"Is that what you'd tell them?" she asked quietly.

"If they asked."

"And would you mean it?"

The question hung between us like a challenge. I could have deflected, could have reminded her this was all pretend.

Instead, I stepped closer. Close enough to see the gold flecks in her brown eyes. Close enough to catch that faint scent of vanilla and antiseptic that was purely her.

"Clara," I said, and my voice came out rougher than I'd intended.

"Yeah?"

"Saturday. You still want to do this?"

She nodded, but her eyes were locked on my mouth. "I want it more than I should."


## CLARA

I spent the rest of the day in a panic.

First about the ceremony—what to wear, what to say, how to act like a bride instead of a woman making a desperate deal.

Then about how real Eli had felt when he'd stepped close outside the courthouse, the way his voice had gone rough when he'd asked if I still wanted to do this.

By evening, I was wondering if I'd be able to let go after this ended. If I'd be able to walk away from whatever this was becoming.

My phone buzzed with a text from Eli: *Can you come by? Need to discuss Saturday.*

I was in my truck before I'd fully processed the decision to go.

Eli opened the door before I knocked, and I caught that now-familiar mix of soap and pine and something darker that was just him.

"Hey," he said.

"Hey." I stepped inside, immediately feeling the warmth wrap around me. "You said we needed to discuss Saturday?"

"Right." But he was looking at me like he'd forgotten what he wanted to say. "Have you eaten?"

"I'm not hungry."

"You're always hungry."

The casual observation made something flutter in my chest. How did he know that about me already?

"I made chili," he said. "It's good."

Twenty minutes later, I was sitting at his kitchen table with a bowl of the best chili I'd ever tasted, watching him move around his kitchen with easy confidence.

"This is incredible," I said. "Where did you learn to cook?"

"Trial and error. Gets boring eating out of cans every night."

"Have you lived alone a lot?"

Something shuttered in his expression. "Yeah."

"By choice?"

He was quiet for a long moment. "Mostly."

I wanted to push, but the careful distance in his voice warned me off. Instead, I focused on the chili and the way he kept glancing at me when he thought I wasn't looking.

"About Saturday," he said finally.

"What about it?"

"The kiss."

My spoon stopped halfway to my mouth. "What about it?"

"We should probably practice."

The words hit me like a physical blow. "Practice?"

"So it looks real. So we don't fumble it in front of everyone."

Of course. For the audience. For the show.

"Right," I said. "That makes sense."

But when he stood up and walked around the table to where I was sitting, when he held out his hand to help me up, it didn't feel like practice.

It felt like a claiming.

"Clara," he said quietly.

I let him pull me to my feet, let him step closer until I had to tilt my head back to meet his eyes.

"This is just practice," I said, but my voice came out breathless.

"Just practice," he agreed.

His hands came up to frame my face, thumbs brushing across my cheekbones. His touch was gentle, careful, like I was something precious.

"Ready?" he asked.

I nodded, not trusting my voice.

He leaned down slowly, giving me time to pull away. I didn't.

His mouth touched mine, soft at first, almost hesitant. Like he was asking permission.

I gave it to him by pressing closer, by letting my hands come up to grip the front of his flannel shirt.

The kiss deepened. His tongue traced my lower lip, and I opened for him with a sound that was definitely not pretend.

When we finally broke apart, we were both breathing hard.

"Good," he said, but his voice was rough. "That should work for Saturday."

My fingers stayed curled in his shirt like I didn't want to let go.

I wasn't sure I did.

"Yeah," I whispered. "Should work."

But as I stood there in his kitchen, his hands still on my face, his eyes dark with something that looked a lot like want, I knew we were both lying.

Nothing about that kiss had been practice.

And Saturday was going to change everything.

# 4

---

# THE RING

E LI

I'd been staring at the same piece of rebar for three hours.

It sat on my workbench in the barn behind the cabin, a chunk of steel salvaged from the old bridge project up on Mill Creek. The same bridge where Mae had pulled my sister from the water twenty years ago.

Seemed fitting.

The forge was already hot—I'd fired it up before dawn, unable to sleep after that kiss in my kitchen. That kiss that was supposed to be practice but felt like a claiming. Like a promise neither of us was ready to make.

But I was making it anyway. In steel and fire and the kind of work that left permanent marks.

I picked up the rebar and thrust it into the coals, watching the metal glow orange, then white-hot. When it was ready, I pulled it out and started hammering, each strike echoing off the barn walls like a heartbeat.

This wasn't about the fake marriage anymore. This was about the way Clara had looked at me when I'd framed her face with my hands. About the way her breath had caught—like she hadn't meant to want me that much.

About the fact that I wanted to put my ring on her finger and mean every damn word of the vows we'd say on Saturday.

The steel began to take shape under my hammer. Rough at first, but gradually smoothing into something that looked like a promise. Like forever hammered into a circle.

By the time the sun was fully up, I had a ring. Raw iron, slightly uneven, but solid. Real. The kind of thing that would last through anything.

I was holding it up to the light when I heard Clara's truck in the driveway.

## CLARA

Eli's barn door was open when I pulled up, and I could hear the rhythmic ring of hammer on metal echoing across the yard.

I found him at a workbench, shirtless despite the December cold, sweat gleaming on his chest and shoulders. His hair was damp, his jaw set in concentration as he worked something small between his fingers.

He looked up when I approached, and something flickered in his gray eyes. Something that made my breath catch.

"Morning," he said.

"Morning." I nodded toward whatever he was holding. "What are you making?"

He was quiet for a long moment, then held out his hand. In his palm sat a ring. Iron, dark and rough-edged, but beautiful in its simplicity.

"For Saturday," he said.

My throat went tight. "You made me a ring."

"Figured we needed one that looked real."

Real. Like everything else about this that was supposed to be fake but felt more honest than anything else in my life.

I reached for it, but he was already placing it in my hand.

The metal was still warm from his hands, heavy and solid. When I slipped it onto my ring finger, it fit perfectly.

"How did you know my size?" I asked.

"Lucky guess."

But the way he was looking at my hand, at his ring on my finger, didn't look like luck. It looked like intention.

"It's beautiful," I said, and meant it.

"It's rough. Uneven."

"It's perfect."

Something shifted in his expression. "Clara."

"Yeah?"

"Saturday. After the ceremony." He paused, jaw working. "Where are you planning to stay?"

The question hit me like a physical blow. We'd talked about the marriage, the legal requirements, and the town's expectations. But we hadn't talked about after.

"I... I don't know. I hadn't thought about it."

" After we're married, you could move into Mae's cabin. Make it yours."

"By myself?"

"If that's what you want."

But the way he said it, the careful distance in his voice, made me study his face more carefully.

"What if it's not?" I said, watching his face.

His hands stilled on the workbench. "What do you want?"

The question hung between us like a dare. I could have deflected, could have reminded him this was all pretend.

Instead, I stepped closer. Close enough to see the sweat beading on his chest, to catch the scent of hot metal and smoke that clung to his skin.

"I want to know why you're really doing this," I said.

"I told you—"

"The truth, Eli. Not the story about Mae and your sister. The real reason."

He was quiet for so long, I thought he wouldn't answer. Then he set down his tools and turned to face me fully.

"You want the truth?"

I nodded.

"The truth is I've been half-dead for three years. Just going through the motions, working and sleeping and pretending it was enough." His voice was rough, honest. "Then you asked me to marry you, and for the first time in three years, I felt like I had a reason to be alive."

The words hit me like a physical blow. "Eli."

"That's not your problem to solve. But you asked for the truth."

I stared at him—at this man who'd been carrying so much pain, who'd somehow found a reason to hope in my desperate proposal.

"What happened three years ago?" I asked.

His jaw clenched. "Lost my crew. Forest fire that went wrong. I was lead sawyer, supposed to keep them safe." He looked away. "Three good men died because I made the wrong call."

The weight of it settled between us like a physical presence. Now I understood the careful distance, the way he lived alone, the photo turned face-down on his refrigerator. The photo of his crew. The men he couldn't save.

"I'm sorry," I said.

"Are you?"

"Yes. And I'm sorry you've been carrying that alone."

He looked back at me then, and something raw and vulnerable flickered in his eyes. "Clara."

"Yeah?"

"This marriage. Whatever it is, whatever it becomes." He paused. "I need you to know it's not just about helping you anymore."

My heart did something strange in my chest. "What's it about?"

"It's about you. About the way you look at me like I'm worth something. About the way you fit in my kitchen, in my life." His voice dropped. "About the way you taste when I kiss you."

The last words came out rough, loaded with want, and I felt heat pool low in my stomach.

"Eli," I whispered.

"I know it's supposed to be fake. I know we agreed on no expectations." He stepped closer, close enough that I had to tilt my head back to meet his eyes. "I want this to be real. All of it. You. Me. The ring. The bed. The damn wedding." He exhaled hard. "Clara, I'm already halfway in love with you and it's killing me not to touch you like I mean it."

The confession hit me like a physical blow. Raw. Honest. Everything I'd been afraid to hope for.

"Then touch me like you mean it," I said.

I reached up and touched his face, felt the scratch of stubble under my palm.

WE KISSED IN HIS BARN, surrounded by the smell of hot metal and sawdust.

This time, there was no pretense about practice, no lies about it being for show. This was real and desperate and honest in a way that made my knees weak.

His hands tangled in my hair, and I pressed closer, needing to feel the solid heat of him against me. When he lifted me onto the workbench, I wrapped my legs around his waist and felt him groan against my mouth.

"Clara," he said, and my name sounded like a prayer.

"I know," I whispered. "I know."

We broke apart breathing hard, foreheads pressed together, the weight of what we'd just admitted settling around us.

"Saturday," he said.

"Saturday."

"After the ceremony, you'll come home with me?"

Home. Like his cabin was already mine too.

"Yes," I said.

He smiled then—the first real smile I'd seen from him—and it transformed his entire face.

"Good," he said, pressing another kiss to my mouth. "Because I've been thinking about having you in my bed since the moment you asked me to marry you."

Heat flared through me at his words, at the promise in his voice.

"Just thinking?" I asked.

His eyes darkened. "Dreaming. Planning. Imagining what you'd look like spread out on my sheets."

"Eli." His name came out breathless.

"Soon," he said, and it sounded like a vow. "Saturday."

I nodded, not trusting my voice.

When I finally climbed down from the workbench, the ring caught the light from the barn door. His ring. On my finger. Where it belonged.

"I should go," I said. "I need to find something to wear for the wedding."

"Wear whatever makes you feel beautiful," he said. "You'll be a knockout either way."

As I walked back to my truck, I could feel him watching me. Could feel the weight of the ring on my finger, the promise we'd just made to each other.

I was marrying Eli Hayes because I loved him.

And if I wasn't careful, I'd start believing I could keep him.

# 5

## THE BED

**E**<sup>LI</sup> The storm hit on Friday night.

I'd been watching the weather reports all week, tracking the system that was supposed to bring light snow through the weekend. Light snow that had turned into a full-blown blizzard that would dump two feet by morning.

Which meant the mountain roads would be impassable. Which meant Clara wouldn't be able to get home tonight.

Which meant she'd have to stay here. In my cabin.

I stood at the kitchen window, watching her truck struggle up the driveway through the driving snow. She'd come by to finalize wedding details—what time, where to meet Nash, what to do if the weather got bad.

Now we had our answer.

The door burst open, and Clara stumbled in on a gust of wind and snow, shaking ice from her hair.

"Holy shit," she said, wrestling the door closed behind her. "When did it get this bad?"

"About an hour ago." I helped her out of her coat, trying not to notice the way her sweater clung to her curves. "Roads are already getting sketchy."

She pulled out her phone, frowned at the screen. "No signal."

"Tower's probably iced over."

"So I'm stuck?"

"Looks like it."

We stared at each other for a long moment, the weight of what that meant settling between us. Clara sleeping here when we both admitted this wasn't going to be some cut and dry fake wedding. Clara in my space for the entire night. Clara twenty feet away from my bed while I tried to pretend I wasn't dying to put my hands on her.

"Couch is comfortable," I said finally.

"Right. The couch."

But neither of us moved toward the living room.

"You hungry?" I asked, because cooking was something I could do with my hands that didn't involve touching her.

"Starving."

I made steaks and roasted vegetables while Clara sat at the kitchen table, the ring I'd forged catching the light every time she moved her hands. She was nervous—I could tell by the way she kept twisting it around her finger.

"Second thoughts?" I asked.

"About the wedding?"

"About staying here tonight."

She looked up at me, and something flickered in her brown eyes. "Are you having second thoughts?"

"No." The word came out rougher than I'd intended. "But Clara, you being here, sleeping twenty feet away from me the night before we get married..."

"What about it?"

I set down the spatula and turned to face her. "I told you I was halfway in love with you. That was yesterday. Today I'm all the way gone."

Her breath caught. "Eli."

"I'm just saying. If you sleep on that couch tonight, I'm going to spend the entire night thinking about carrying you to my bed. About what you'd look like spread out on my sheets. About all the ways I want to touch you after we say those vows tomorrow."

Heat flared in her eyes. "And that's a problem because?"

"Because if I touch you tonight, I won't stop."

She stood up slowly, walked around the table until she was close enough to touch. "What if I don't want you to keep your hands to yourself?"

My hands clenched into fists at my sides. "Clara."

"What if I've been thinking the same things? What if I've been imagining what it would feel like to have you touch me like you mean it?"

"Don't."

"Don't what?"

"Don't make this harder than it already is."

She reached up and touched my face, and I couldn't stop myself from leaning into her palm.

"Tomorrow we get married," she said quietly. "Tomorrow I become your wife, even if it's just on paper. Tonight I'm just Clara, and you're just Eli, and we're snowed in together."

"Just Clara and Eli," I repeated.

"Just us."

I stared down at her—at this woman who'd asked me to marry her and somehow made me fall in love with her in the process— and felt my resolve cracking.

"The couch," I said.

"The couch," she agreed.

But when she went up on her toes and kissed me, soft and sweet and full of promise, I knew she wouldn't be sleeping on the couch tonight.


## CLARA

We made it through dinner without touching each other.

Barely.

Every time Eli moved around the kitchen, I was hyperaware of his presence. The way his jeans hugged his thighs. The way his flannel stretched across his shoulders. The way he kept looking at me like he was fighting the urge to crowd me against the nearest wall.

By the time we finished eating, the tension in the cabin was thick enough to cut.

"Storm's getting worse," Eli said, checking the window.

"How much worse?"

"Bad enough that even if the roads clear by morning, we might not make it to town for the ceremony."

My heart stopped. "What do you mean?"

"I mean we might have to postpone."

"No." The word came out sharper than I'd intended. "No, we can't postpone. The deadline is Christmas Day. If we don't get married soon—"

"Hey." Eli crossed to where I was standing, put his hands on my shoulders. "We'll figure it out. Nash has a four-wheel drive. Worst case, he comes here."

"Here?"

"Why not? We get married in front of the fireplace. Just us and Nash. Simple."

The idea of marrying Eli in his cabin, in front of the fire where we'd shared so many quiet moments, made something warm unfurl in my chest.

"You'd be okay with that?" I asked.

"Clara, I'd marry you in a snowbank if that's what it took."

The intensity in his voice made my breath catch. "Eli."

"I'm serious. Tomorrow, next week, next month—I don't care when or where. I just want to call you my wife."

The words slammed into me. "Even though it's supposed to be temporary?"

Something shifted in his expression. "Is it?"

"Is it what?"

"Temporary."

I stared up at him, at this man who'd become everything to me in less than a week, and felt the last of my defenses crumble.

"I don't want it to be," I whispered.

"Good," he said, and then he was kissing me.

This kiss was different from the others. Deeper. More desperate. Like we were both drowning and this was our only source of air.

When we finally broke apart, we were both breathing hard.

"Clara," he said, and my name sounded like a prayer.

"I know."

"If we do this—if we cross this line—there's no going back."

"I don't want to go back."

He studied my face for a long moment, like he was memorizing every detail. Then he took my hand and led me toward his bedroom.

The room was simple, masculine. A king-size bed dominated the space, covered with a dark quilt that looked handmade. Moonlight filtered through the window, casting everything in silver.

"You sure?" he asked.

Instead of answering, I reached for the hem of my sweater and pulled it over my head.

Eli's breath caught. His eyes tracked the lace, the curve of my waist, the way I breathed like I already belonged to him.

"Beautiful," he said, and the reverence in his voice made me feel like a goddess.

I reached for him then, started unbuttoning his flannel with shaking fingers. He stood perfectly still, letting me undress him, his gray eyes never leaving my face.

When I pushed the shirt off his shoulders, I had to bite back a gasp. He was all muscle and scars, broad shoulders tapering to a narrow waist. A line of dark hair disappeared beneath his jeans.

I let my hands explore his chest, tracing the scars, learning the feel of him. When I leaned forward and pressed a kiss to his collarbone, he groaned.

"Clara."

"I want you," I said against his skin. "I want this. I want us."

He lifted me then, laid me down on his bed like I was something precious. The quilt was soft beneath me, warm from the heat of his body.

"We should wait," he said, but his hands were already skimming over my skin. "Until after the wedding."

"Why?"

"Because you deserve—"

I silenced him with a kiss. "I deserve you. And you deserve to be happy. We both do."

He stared down at me for a long moment, then reached behind me to unhook my bra. When he pulled it away, his eyes darkened with want.

"Christ, you're perfect."

He kissed me then, his mouth traveling from my lips to my throat to the sensitive spot where my neck met my shoulder.

When he took my breast in his mouth, I arched beneath him with a cry.

"Eli, please."

"Please what?"

"Touch me. All of me."

His hands skimmed lower, finding the waistband of my jeans. "Here?"

"Everywhere."


## ELI

I'd imagined this moment a hundred times since the day I met her.

Clara in my bed. Clara beneath me. Clara saying my name like a prayer.

But nothing I'd imagined came close to the reality.

She was soft and warm and responsive, her body arching into my touch like she'd been made for me. When I stripped away the last of her clothes and finally had her naked beneath me, I had to stop and just look.

"What?" she asked, suddenly self-conscious.

"You're perfect," I said, and meant it. Every curve, every freckle, every inch of skin that I wanted to worship with my mouth and hands.

I kissed my way down her body, taking my time, learning what made her gasp and moan and whisper my name. When I settled between her thighs, she looked down at me with eyes dark with want.

"Eli."

"Let me," I said. "Let me take care of you."

I used my mouth and tongue until she was writhing beneath me, her hands fisted in my hair, her body tight with need. When she finally came apart, crying out my name, I felt like I'd conquered the world.

"Come here," she said, pulling me up to kiss her. "I need you inside me."

I reached for my wallet, found the condom I'd been carrying like an optimist. When I moved over her, she wrapped her legs around my waist and guided me home.

The first slide into her heat nearly undid me. She was tight and wet and perfect, and I had to grit my teeth to keep from finishing before we'd even started.

"Okay?" I asked.

"More than okay." She lifted her hips, taking me deeper. "Move, Eli. Please."

I moved then, setting a rhythm that had us both gasping. She met me thrust for thrust, her nails digging into my shoulders, her mouth hot against my neck.

"I love you," I said against her ear, the words torn from somewhere deep inside me.

"I love you too," she gasped. "God, Eli, I love you so much."

We moved together like we'd been doing this for years instead of the first time. Like our bodies had been waiting for this moment, this connection, this perfect joining.

When Clara came , her body clenching around me like a fist, I followed her over the edge with a groan that sounded like her name.

Afterward, we lay tangled together, her head on my chest, my fingers tracing patterns on her bare shoulder.

"So," she said eventually.

"So."

"That happened."

"It did."

She lifted her head to look at me. "Any regrets?"

I brushed a strand of hair from her face. "Just one."

Her face fell. "What?"

"That we waited this long."

She laughed, the sound bright and joyful in the quiet room. "We've known each other for six days."

"Longest six days of my life."

She kissed my chest, right over my heart. "What happens now?"

"Now we get married. For real this time."

"For real?"

"Clara." I tilted her chin up so she had to meet my eyes. "That ring on your finger? The vows we're saying tomorrow? The way I feel about you? None of it's fake anymore."

"None of it?"

"Not a damn bit."

She smiled then, the kind of smile that could stop wars and start them. "Good. Because I was never very good at pretending anyway."

Outside, the storm raged on. But inside, wrapped around the woman I loved, I'd never felt more at peace.

Tomorrow we'd get married.

Tonight, she was already mine.

# 6

## THE VOWS

CLARA

I woke up in Eli's arms.

The window was pale with morning. Cold against the glass, warm in his bed. His chest rose and fell beneath my cheek, steady and reassuring, and for a moment, I let myself pretend this was just another Saturday morning in a life we'd built together.

Then I remembered. Today was our wedding day.

"You awake?" Eli's voice was rough with sleep.

"Mmm." I pressed a kiss to his chest. "How long have you been up?"

"Few minutes. Watching you sleep."

I lifted my head to look at him. His hair was messed up, stubble dark on his jaw, gray eyes soft in a way I'd never seen before.

"Any regrets?" I asked.

"About last night?" He traced a finger down my spine, making me shiver. "Not a single one."

"About today?"

His hand stilled. "What do you mean?"

"The wedding. Marrying me for real instead of fake."

He was quiet for a moment, and something cold settled in my stomach. Then he rolled us over, pinning me beneath him, his eyes intense.

"Clara," he said. "The only regret I have is that we didn't do this sooner."

Relief flooded through me. "Good. Because I love you, and I want to marry you, and I don't care if that makes me crazy."

"It makes you mine," he said, and kissed me until I couldn't remember why I'd been worried. Even the weather was collaborating. The storm seemed to be clearing up.

An hour later, we were dressed and drinking coffee when Nash's truck pulled into the driveway.

"He made it," I said, peering out the window.

"Course he did. Nash doesn't let a little snow stop him from anything."

Nash knocked once and walked in, stomping his boots on the mat. He was a big man with graying hair and kind eyes, the kind of person who looked like he could handle any crisis.

"Morning, lovebirds," he said, grinning. "Ready to make this official?"

"Ready," Eli said, and the certainty in his voice made my chest tight.

"Good. Because I've got about six people in town asking when they can come congratulate you." Nash accepted the coffee Eli offered him. "Dolores has been calling everyone since yesterday, telling them about the romantic Christmas wedding."

My palms went cold. I almost stepped back. "But what if they ask questions? What if they want details about how we met, how long we've been together?"

"Hey." He crossed to where I was standing, put his hands on my shoulders. "It's fine. We'll do exactly what we planned. Nash will marry us, we'll kiss, and everyone will congratulate us."

Nash was watching us with interest. "You two okay? You seem nervous for people who've been together long enough to get married."

Heat flooded my cheeks. "We're fine. Just... wedding jitters."

"Normal," Nash said. "I've married a lot of couples over the years. They all get nervous right before."

"How many couples?" I asked.

"Dozens. And you know what? The ones who are nervous usually last the longest. Means they understand what they're promising."

I met Eli's eyes across the kitchen. Did we understand what we were promising? Or were we still figuring it out as we went?

"So," Nash said, setting down his coffee. "Where do you want to do this?"


ELI

We decided on the living room, in front of the fireplace.

Nash moved the coffee table out of the way while I built up the fire. Clara disappeared into the bedroom to get ready, and I tried not to think about how she'd looked this morning—sleepy and soft and mine.

Twenty minutes later, she emerged in a simple blue dress that hugged her curves and made her eyes look like warm honey. She'd braided her hair to one side, and she was wearing the ring I'd forged for her.

She looked like something carved straight from the life I didn't think I'd ever get to have. Real. Sure of herself. Mine.

"You clean up nice," I said.

"So do you."

I'd put on my best flannel and clean jeans, nothing fancy. But the way Clara was looking at me made me feel like I was wearing a tuxedo.

"You ready?" Nash asked.

We stood in front of the fireplace, Nash between us and the fire crackling behind him. Through the window, I could see snow still falling, but lighter now. The storm had passed.

"Before we start," Nash said, "I need to ask. You both understand what you're doing here? Marriage isn't something to take lightly."

"We understand," I said.

Clara nodded. "We do."

"Good. Because I've known you, Clara, since you were knee-high, and, Eli, I've known you since you joined the trail crew, and I've never seen either of you look at another person the way you're looking at each other right now."

My chest tightened. Nash was right. I'd never felt about anyone the way I felt about Clara. Never wanted to protect and claim and cherish someone so completely.

"Clara," Nash said. "Do you take Eli to be your husband? To have and to hold, for better or worse, for richer or poorer, in sickness and in health, for as long as you both shall live?"

Clara's eyes never left mine. "I do."

"Eli, do you take Clara to be your wife? To have and to hold, for better or worse, for richer or poorer, in sickness and in health, for as long as you both shall live?"

"I do," I said, and meant every word.

"Rings?"

I pulled the iron band from my pocket—the mate to the one Clara was wearing. I'd forged it this morning while she slept, a simple band that matched hers.

"With this ring," I said, sliding it onto my finger, "I thee wed."

Clara's eyes were bright with tears. "With this ring," she said, touching the band already on her finger, "I thee wed."

"By the power vested in me by the state of Montana," Nash said, "I now pronounce you husband and wife." He grinned. "You may kiss your bride."

I stepped closer to Clara, framed her face with my hands the way I had that first night in my kitchen. But this time, when I kissed her, it wasn't practice.

It was a promise.

Her lips were soft under mine, warm and willing. She kissed me like she needed it, like I was air and she'd been holding her breath too long. I deepened the kiss, forgetting about Nash, forgetting about everything except the woman in my arms.

We finally broke apart, when Nash coughed.

"Well," Nash said, clearing his throat. "That was... thorough."

Clara laughed, her cheeks flushed. "Sorry."

"Don't apologize. That's how you kiss your wife." Nash clapped me on the shoulder. "Congratulations, you two. May you have many happy years together."

Many happy years. I wanted that more than I'd ever wanted anything.

"Thank you," Clara said. "For everything."

"My pleasure. And Clara? Welcome to the family."

After Nash left, Clara and I stood in the living room looking at each other. Married. Actually married.

"So," she said. "How does it feel?"

"How does what feel?"

"Being married."

I stepped closer, pulled her into my arms. "Feels right. Feels like I've been waiting my whole life for this moment."

"Even though it started as fake?"

"Especially because it started as fake." I kissed her forehead. "Means we chose this. Chose each other. No pressure, no expectations. Just us deciding we wanted to be together."

She smiled up at me. "I love you, husband."

"I love you too, wife."


**CLARA**

We were eating breakfast when the first car pulled into the driveway.

"Who's that?" I asked, peering out the window.

Eli looked over my shoulder. "Dolores. And it looks like she brought company."

Three more cars followed, and soon the yard was full of people I recognized from town. Dolores, of course. The Hendersons from the feed store. Sarah and Mike from the diner. Even Dr. Brennan, who had graciously given be a job at his the vet clinic while I get mine going.

"Shit," I muttered.

"Hey." Eli turned me to face him. "We can do this. We just got married. We're happy. That's all they need to see."

"But what if—"

He silenced me with a kiss. Quick, sure, claiming. "Trust me."

The knock came before I could answer.

Eli opened the door to find Dolores holding a casserole dish and beaming.

"Congratulations!" she said, pushing past him into the cabin. "We couldn't let you have a wedding without a proper celebration."

The rest of the group followed, filling the small space with chatter and laughter. Someone had brought champagne. Someone else had cake. In minutes, our quiet morning had turned into a party.

"Clara, dear," Dolores said, pulling me aside. "You look absolutely radiant. Marriage suits you."

"Thank you."

"And Eli seems so happy. I've never seen him smile so much." She lowered her voice conspiratorially. "How long have you two really been together? Because this all seems very sudden."

My heart jumped. I looked at the door. Thought about running. "We—"

"Sometimes it happens fast," Eli said, appearing at my side. His arm went around my waist, pulling me close. "When you know, you know."

"Oh, how romantic!" Dolores clasped her hands together. "Just like in the movies."

Dr. Brennan approached with a glass of champagne. "Clara, I have to say, I'm surprised. You never mentioned you were seeing anyone."

Heat flooded my cheeks. "It was... private."

"Well, I'm happy for you. You deserve someone who appreciates you." He turned to Eli. "You're a lucky man."

"I know," Eli said, and the possessive edge in his voice made my pulse skip.

The party continued around us, but I was hyperaware of Eli's presence. The way he kept his hand on me—my waist, my back, my shoulder. The way he introduced me as "my wife" like he'd been doing it for years. The way he looked at me when he thought no one was watching, like I was something precious he couldn't quite believe was his.

It felt real. All of it.

"Speech!" someone called out.

"Yes, speech!" others joined in.

Eli's arm tightened around me. "What do you want to hear?"

"How you knew Clara was the one," Sarah called out.

"When you decided to propose," Mike added.

I looked up at Eli, panic rising. But Eli just smiled, that slow, devastating smile that made my knees weak.

"Easy," he said, loud enough for everyone to hear. "The moment she asked me to marry her."

Laughter filled the room, but Eli's eyes were serious as they met mine.

"She was sitting on a sidewalk, crying because life had knocked her down. And instead of staying down, she got up and asked for help. Asked me to be part of her solution." His voice dropped, became more intimate despite the audience. "That's when I knew. Clara Chen doesn't give up. And I wanted to be the man standing beside her when she conquers the world."

The room went quiet. Someone sniffled.

"Plus," Eli added, grinning, "she makes the best coffee I've ever had."

Everyone laughed, but I barely heard them. I was staring up at my husband, this man who'd just told our entire story in a way that was completely true and completely safe.

He'd protected us. Protected me.

Without thinking, I reached up and kissed him. Hard. In front of everyone.

When we broke apart, the room erupted in cheers and whistles.

"Beautiful!" Dolores called out, dabbing at her eyes with a tissue.

"What was that for?" he asked quietly.

"For being perfect," I said. "For protecting us. For making this real."

"It was always real, Clara. From the moment you asked."

Looking up at him, surrounded by friends and neighbors celebrating our marriage, I finally believed him.

This wasn't fake anymore. Maybe it never had been.

This was love. This was forever.

This was ours.

# 7

# THE WEDDING

C LARA

    The last guest left at sunset.

    I stood in the doorway, watching taillights disappear down the mountain road, and felt something settle in my chest. Peace. Contentment. The quiet satisfaction of a day that had gone exactly right.

Behind me, Eli was cleaning up—stacking plates, gathering empty champagne glasses, moving through his cabin like the efficient man he was. But I could feel his attention on me even with his back turned.

"They're gone," I said.

"Good." His voice was rough. "I was about ready to start throwing people out."

I turned to look at him. "Why?"

"Because I've been wanting to get my hands on my wife all day."

The word 'wife' sent heat straight through me. Legal now. Official. Real in every way that mattered.

"Your wife," I repeated, testing the sound of it.

"My wife." He set down the glasses and moved toward me with deliberate intent. "Mrs. Hayes."

"I like the sound of that."

"Good. Because you're stuck with it."

When he reached me, his hands came up to frame my face the way they had during our ceremony. But this time, there was no audience. No one to perform for.

Just us.

"Clara Hayes," he said quietly.

"Eli Hayes," I said back.

"How does it feel?"

"Like coming home."

He kissed me then, slow and deep and thorough. When we broke apart, we were both breathing hard.

"Bedroom," he said. "Now."

"Demanding."

"You have no idea."


## ELI

I'd been thinking about this moment all day.

Clara in my bed as my wife. Clara beneath me with my ring on her finger and my name legally hers. Clara making those sounds she made when I touched her just right.

But first, I had something to give her.

"Wait," I said when we reached the bedroom.

"Wait?" She looked at me like I'd lost my mind. "Eli, if you're having second thoughts now—"

"Not second thoughts." I went to the dresser, pulled out the small wrapped box I'd hidden there this morning. "Wedding present."

Her eyes went wide. "You got me a wedding present?"

"Open it."

She unwrapped it carefully, like the paper mattered. Inside was a simple silver chain with a small pendant—a tiny hammer, forged from the same iron as our rings.

"It's beautiful," she whispered.

"Thought you should have something that represents how we started. You asking for help. Me building something for you."

"Will you put it on me?"

I lifted her hair, fastened the chain around her neck. The pendant settled just above her cleavage, catching the light.

"Perfect," I said.

"Your turn." She went to her purse, pulled out a small box. "I got you something too."

Inside was a simple leather bracelet with a single metal plate. Engraved on it were coordinates.

"What is this?" I asked.

"The exact spot where we met. Where you said yes." Her voice was soft. "So you'll always remember the moment our life together started."

I stared at the bracelet, throat tight. "Clara."

"Do you like it?"

"I love it. I love you." I fastened it around my wrist, next to my watch. "Thank you."

"Thank you for saying yes that day."

"Thank you for asking."

We stood there for a moment, just looking at each other. My wife. My beautiful, brave, stubborn wife who'd saved us both.

"Now," I said, stepping closer. "Where were we?"

"You were about to make love to your wife."

"Mrs. Hayes."

"That's me."

I reached for the zipper of her dress, pulled it down slowly. The blue fabric pooled at her feet, leaving her in lace and skin and the pendant I'd given her.

"I'm never gonna get used to the way you look at me like that."

"So are you."

Her hands went to my shirt, fingers working the buttons with more confidence than that first night. When she pushed it off my shoulders, she pressed kisses to my chest, my collarbone, the sensitive spot at the base of my throat.

"Clara."

"I love you," she said against my skin. "My husband."

I lifted her then, laid her on the bed that was ours now. Not mine, not hers. Ours.

"I love you too," I said, settling over her. "My wife."

## CLARA

Making love as husband and wife felt different.

More intense. More claiming. Like every touch was a promise, every kiss a vow we hadn't spoken in front of Nash but meant just the same.

Eli took his time, worshipping my body with his hands and mouth until I was shaking beneath him. When he finally joined with me, it felt like coming home and setting out on an adventure all at once.

"Mine," he said against my ear.

"Yours," I agreed. "Always yours."

We moved together with the rhythm of people who'd found their match. When I came apart in his arms, crying out his name, he followed me over the edge with a groan that sounded like relief.

Afterward, we lay tangled together, sweat cooling on our skin, hearts still racing.

"We're married."

"We are."

"For real."

"For real," I repeated.

I traced patterns on his chest, feeling the steady beat of his heart under my palm. "What happens now?"

"Now?" He tightened his arms around me. "Now we go to sleep in our bed, in our cabin, and tomorrow we start figuring out our life together."

"Our cabin?"

"You belong here, Clara. With me."

The certainty in his voice made my chest tight. "What about the clinic? My job?"

"Set up in Mae's barn like you planned. I'll help you build whatever you need."

"You'd do that?"

"I'd do anything for you. Build you a clinic, renovate the barn, drive you to town every day if that's what you wanted." He tilted my chin up so I had to meet his eyes. "But I think you want to be here. I think you want to build something with me."

He was right. I did want that. Wanted to wake up every morning in his arms, wanted to build a veterinary practice on the land that was legally mine now, wanted to make a life with this man who'd saved me in every way that mattered.

"Yes," I said. "I want to build something with you."

"Good. Because I've got plans."

"What kind of plans?"

"Big ones. The barn needs work. The fencing needs repair. And I'm thinking we need to expand the cabin."

"Expand it?"

"More bedrooms." His hand settled on my hip, possessive and warm. "For when we're ready."

The implication hit me like lightning. "Eli."

"Too soon to talk about kids?"

"We've been married for less than twelve hours."

"We've been in love longer than that."

He was right. I'd been falling for him since that first night in his kitchen, maybe even since he'd offered to marry me on that sidewalk.

"Not too soon," I said quietly. "Someday."

"Someday." He pressed a kiss to my forehead. "I can work with someday."

I curled closer to him, breathing in the scent of soap and pine and satisfaction that clung to his skin. Through the window, snow was falling again, but gently this time. Not a storm, just a soft blanket settling over our mountain.

"Eli?"

"Yeah?"

"Thank you."

"For what?"

"For saying yes. For making this real. For loving me enough to build a forever."

"Clara." His voice was rough with emotion. "Thank you for asking. For being brave enough to take a chance on a broken-down sawyer with too much baggage."

"You're not broken down."

"I was. Before you."

I lifted my head to look at him. "And now?"

"Now I'm exactly where I'm supposed to be."


ELI

I woke up on Christmas morning with my wife in my arms.

Clara was still sleeping, her hair spread across my chest, one hand resting over my heart. Sunrise hit the window. The pendant I'd given her caught the glow, and the ring I'd forged gleamed on her finger.

My wife. My Clara. The woman who'd saved me by asking me to save her.

Outside, the world was white and perfect. Inside, everything I'd ever wanted was right here in my bed.

Clara stirred, made a soft sound of contentment, and pressed closer.

"Morning, husband," she said without opening her eyes.

"Morning, wife."

"Merry Christmas."

"Merry Christmas."

She lifted her head to look at me, eyes soft with sleep and love. "Any regrets?"

"About marrying you? Not a single one."

"About the fake marriage that turned real?"

"Best fake marriage ever."

She laughed, the sound bright and joyful in the quiet room. "I love you, Eli Hayes."

"I love you too, Clara Hayes."

Outside, Christmas morning was breaking over the mountains. Inside, we were building something that would last longer than any storm, stronger than any doubt.

We were building forever.

And it started with a desperate woman asking a stranger to marry her, and a lonely man saying yes.

Sometimes the best things begin with the worst plans.

Sometimes salvation comes disguised as a favor.

Sometimes love finds you when you're not even looking for it.

And sometimes, if you're very lucky, the person you marry for all the wrong reasons turns out to be exactly the right person to spend the rest of your life with.

I was very lucky.

We both were.

The End

Did you enjoy *More Mountain Man Trail Builders*?

Please consider reviewing it on Amazon, Goodreads or Bookbub.

Reviews help me reach new readers.

This completes the **Bitteroot Ridge Trail Crew** series.

**Ready for more?**

Read the **Bitteroot Ridge Search and Rescue** series!

Have you read Nash's story?

Read *Rugged Mountain Man* for **FREE**!

*One storm. One cabin. One grumpy trail boss meets his match.*

- POSSESSIVE MOUNTAIN MAN
- CURVY, COMPETENT HEROINE
- ONLY ONE BED
- WRECKED BY THE QUIET ONES
- CARVED NAME, NOTCHED HEART
- HEA GUARANTEED

# ABOUT PEYTON LAWSON

Peyton Lawson writes steamy romance that burns hard and loves harder—Viking warriors, grumpy mountain men, and the curvy heroines who bring them to their knees. Her stories deliver action, emotion, and no-fade heat with guaranteed HEAs. When she's not writing, she's reading, hiking, or chasing her next wild escape.

www.peytonlawsonromance.com

# ALSO BY PEYTON LAWSON

### Bitterroot Ridge Search and Rescue

Redeemed by the Mountain Man (FREE Reader Magnet)

Saved by the Mountain Man

Carried by the Mountain Man

Tracked by the Mountain Man

Stranded with the Mountain Man

Rescued by the Mountain Man

Off-Limits Mountain Man

Sheltered Mountain Man

### Bitterrot Ridge Trail Crew

Rugged Mountain Man (FREE Reader Magnet)

Forbidden Mountain Man

Devoted Mountain Man

Untamed Mountain Man

Irresistible Mountain Man

Relentless Mountain Man

Carved by the Mountain Man

Branded Mountain Man

The Virgin Mountain Man who Falls First

Christmas with the Trail-Building Mountain Man

Christmas Vows for the Mountain Man